#3

Trolls

"Party With The Bergens"

MORE GREAT GRAPHIC NOVEL SERIES AVAILABLE FROM PAPERCUTZ

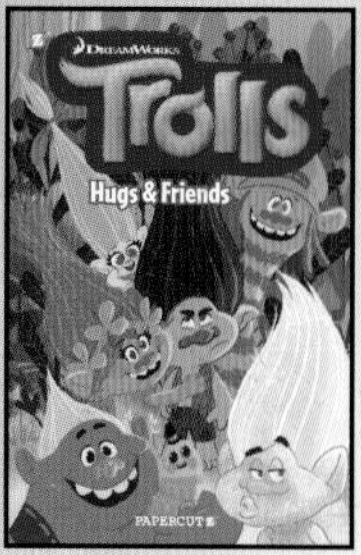
DreamWorks
Trolls
Hugs & Friends
PAPERCUTZ
TROLLS #1

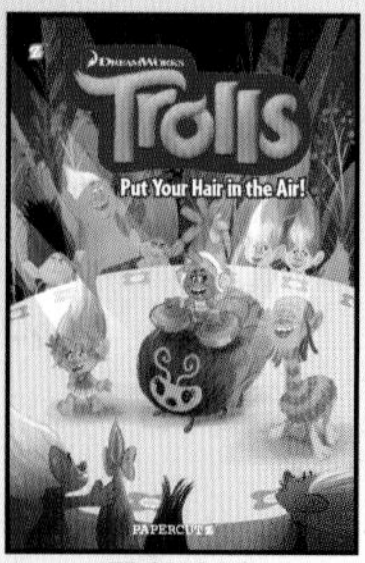
DreamWorks
Trolls
Put Your Hair in the Air!
PAPERCUTZ
TROLLS #2

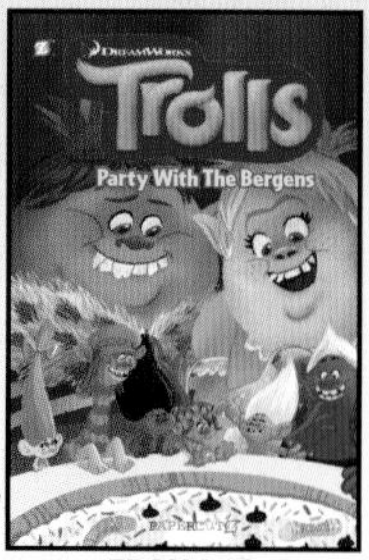
DreamWorks
Trolls
Party With The Bergens
TROLLS #3

COMING SOON

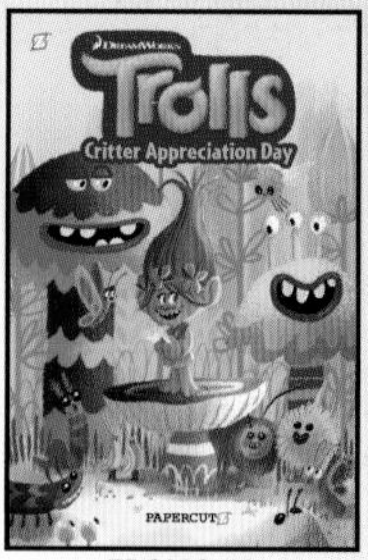
DreamWorks
Trolls
Critter Appreciation Day
PAPERCUTZ
TROLLS #4

COMING SOON

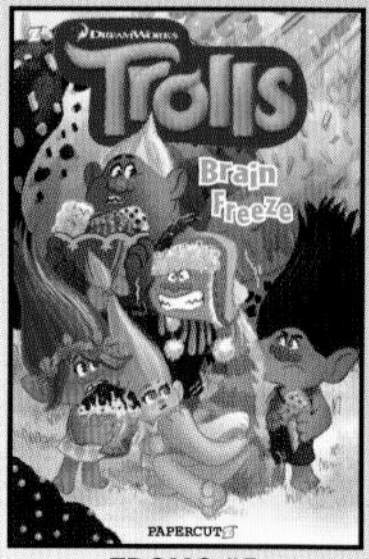
DreamWorks
Trolls
Brain Freeze
PAPERCUTZ
TROLLS #5

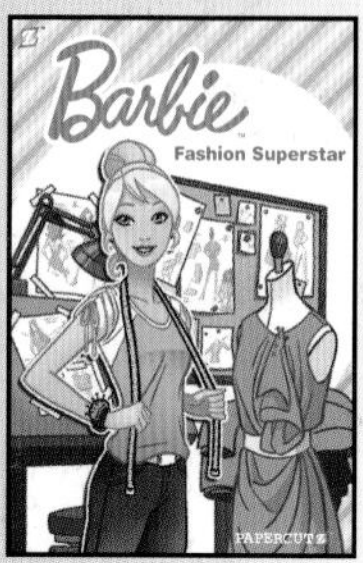
Barbie
Fashion Superstar
PAPERCUTZ
BARBIE #1

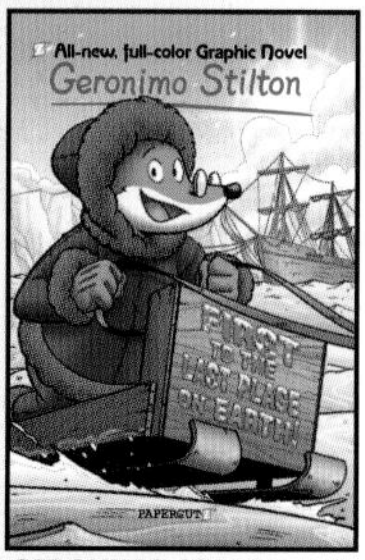
All-new, full-color Graphic Novel
Geronimo Stilton
PAPERCUTZ
GERONIMO STILTON #18

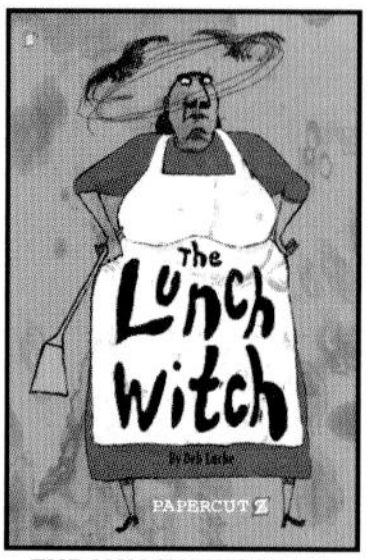
The Lunch Witch
By Deb Lucke
PAPERCUTZ
THE LUNCH WITCH #1

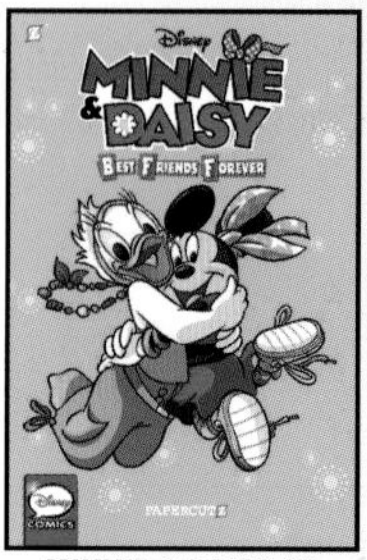
Disney
Minnie & Daisy
Best Friends Forever
PAPERCUTZ
MINNIE & DAISY #1

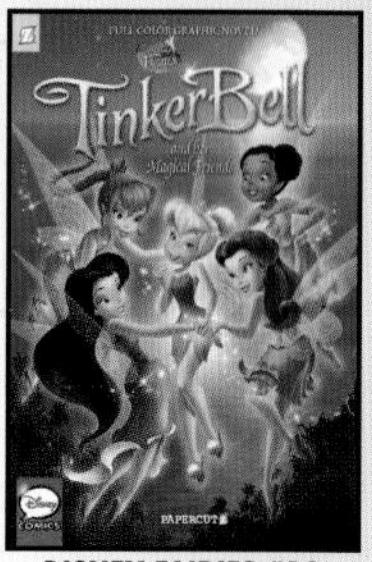
Tinker Bell
PAPERCUTZ
DISNEY FAIRIES #18

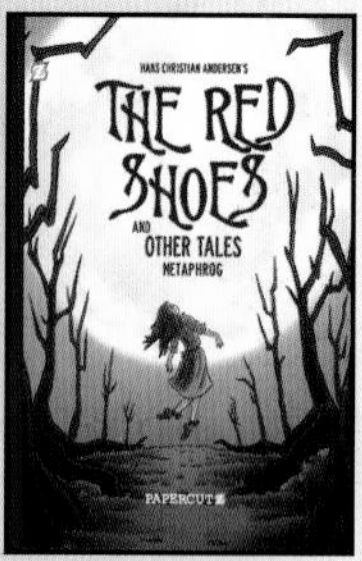
The Red Shoes
and Other Tales
Metaphrog
PAPERCUTZ
THE RED SHOES

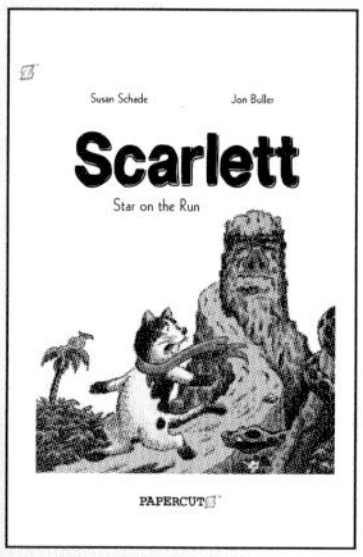
Susan Schade
Jon Buller
Scarlett
Star on the Run
PAPERCUTZ
SCARLETT

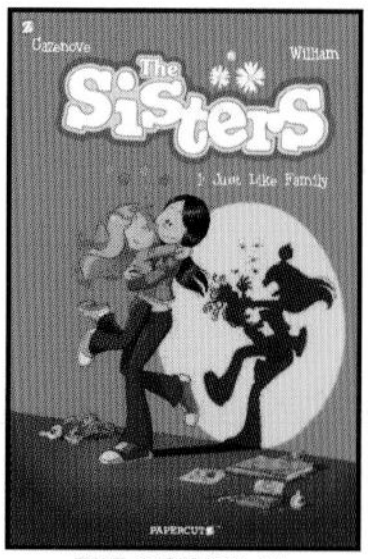
Cazenove
William
The Sisters
PAPERCUTZ
THE SISTERS #1

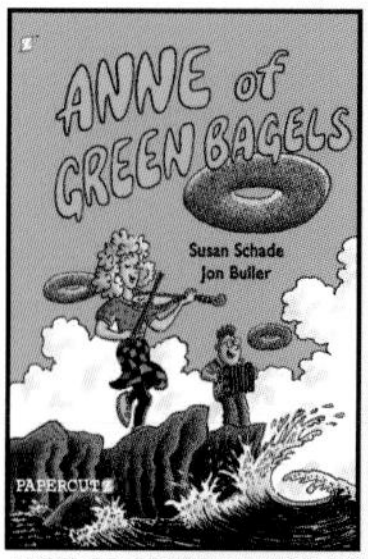
Anne of Green Bagels
Susan Schade
Jon Buller
PAPERCUTZ
ANNE OF GREEN BAGELS #1

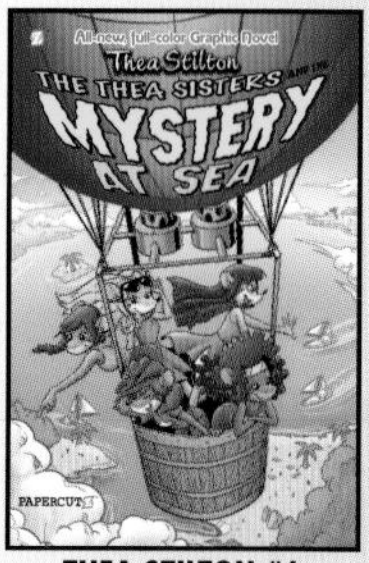
All-new, full-color Graphic Novel
Thea Stilton
The Thea Sisters
Mystery at Sea
PAPERCUTZ
THEA STILTON #6

TROLLS, BARBIE, MINNIE & DAISY, and DISNEY FAIRIES graphic novels are available for $7.99 in paperback, and $12.99 in hardcover. GERONIMO STILTON and THEA STILTON graphic novels are available for $9.99 in hardcover only. THE LUNCH WITCH, SCARLETT, and ANNE OF GREEN BAGELS graphic novels are available for $14.99 in paperback only. THE RED SHOES graphic novel is available for $12.99 in hardcover only. THE SISTERS graphic novels are available for $9.99 in paperback, and $14.99 in hardcover.

Available from booksellers everywhere. You can also order online from www.papercutz.com. Or call 1-800-886-1223, Monday through Friday, 9–5 EST. MC, Visa, and AmEx accepted. To order by mail, please add $5.00 for postage and handling for first book ordered, $1.00 for each additional book and make check payable to NBM Publishing. Send to: Papercutz, 160 Broadway, Suite 700, East Wing, New York, NY 10038.

TROLLS, BARBIE, GERONIMO STILTON, THEA STILTON, THE LUNCH WITCH, THE RED SHOES, SCARLETT, and ANNE OF GREEN BAGELS graphic novels are also available wherever e-books are sold.

DreamWorks Trolls

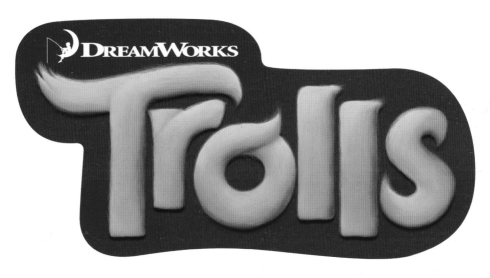

TABLE OF CONTENTS

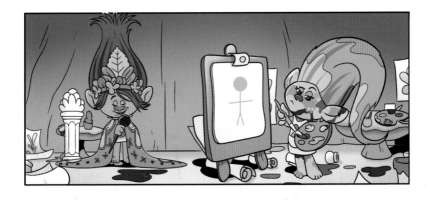

DREAMWORKS

TROLLS

#3

"Party With The Bergens"

"PIZZA PARTY!"
Script: Dave Scheidt
Art and Colors: Kathryn Hudson
Letters: Tom Orzechowski

"TO BE OR NOT TO BE... SOMEBODY ELSE"
Script: Rafał Skarżycki
Art and Colors: Artful Doodlers
Letters: Dawn Guzzo

"RAD"
Script: Dave Scheidt
Art and Colors: Kathryn Hudson
Letters: Tom Orzechowski

"ROYAL PORTRAIT"
Script: Michał Gałek
Pencils and Inks: Miguel Fernandez
Colors: Artful Doodlers
Letters: Dawn Guzzo

"HAIR SCHOOL"
Script: Dave Scheidt
Art and Colors: Kathryn Hudson
Letters: Tom Orzechowski

"BRIDGET 2.0"
Script: Dave Scheidt
Art and Colors: Kathryn Hudson
Letters: Tom Orzechowski

"SECRET MESSENGER"
Script: Michał Gałek
Pencils: Angel Rodriguez
Inks: Ferran Rodriguez
Colors: Artful Doodlers
Letters: Dawn Guzzo

"LISTEN UP!"
Script: Dave Scheidt
Art and Colors: Kathryn Hudson
Letters: Tom Orzechowski

Production — Dawn K. Guzzo
Editor — Robert V. Conte
Assistant Managing Editor — Jeff Whitman
Special Thanks to DreamWorks Animation LLC —
Corinne Combs, Lawrence "Shifty" Hamashima,
Mike Sund, Barbara Layman, Alex Ward, John Tanzer,
and Megan Startz
Jim Salicrup
Editor-in-Chief

ISBN: 978-1-62991-794-8 Paperback Edition
ISBN: 978-1-62991-795-5 Hardcover Edition

Printed in Korea
2017

Papercutz books may be purchased for business or promotional use.
For information on bulk purchases please contact Macmillan Corporate
and Premium Sales Department at (800) 221-7945 x5442.

Distributed by Macmillan
First Printing

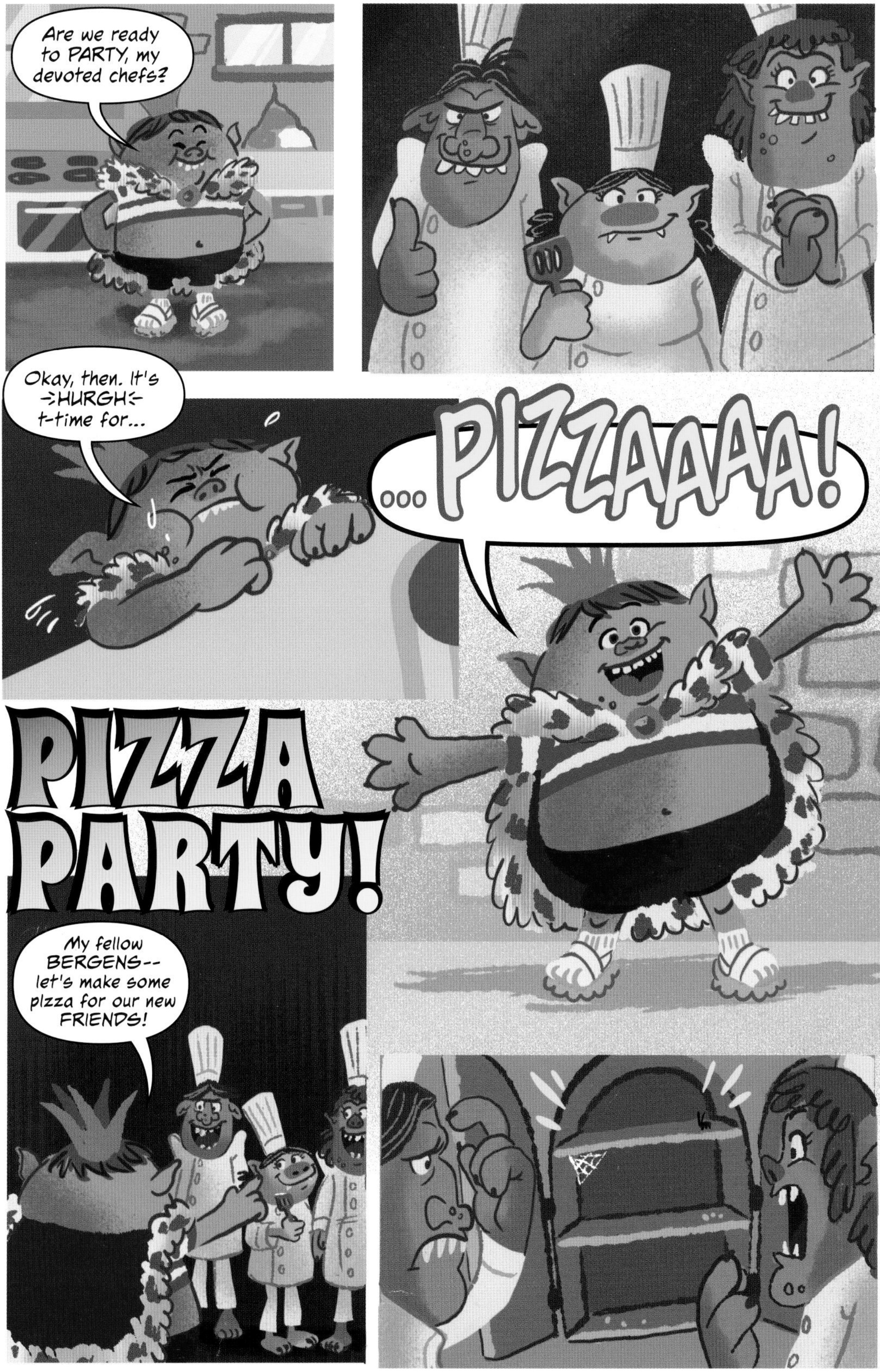
Are we ready to PARTY, my devoted chefs?
Okay, then. It's HURGH t-time for...
...PIZZAAAA!
PIZZA PARTY!
My fellow BERGENS-- let's make some pizza for our new FRIENDS!

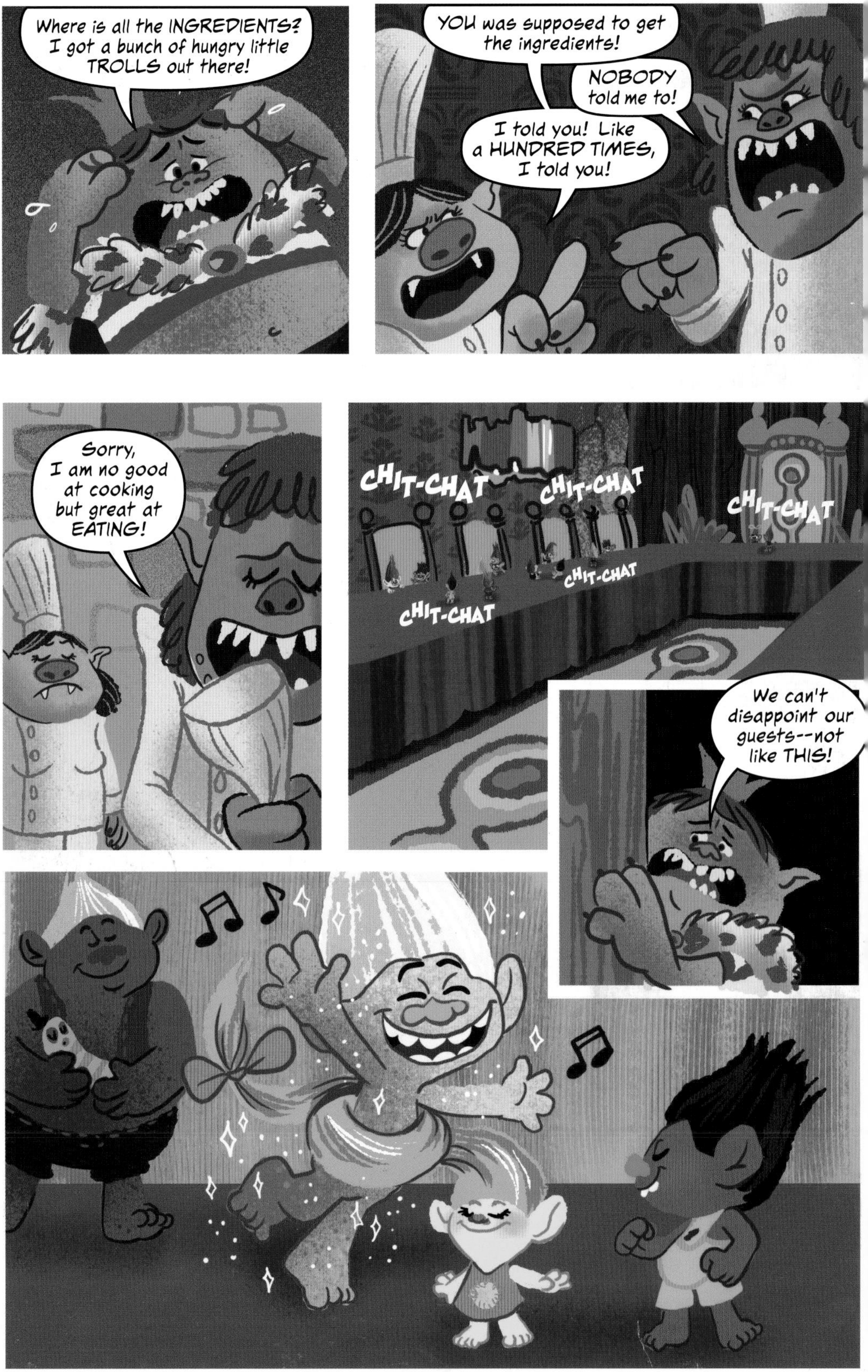
Where is all the INGREDIENTS? I got a bunch of hungry little TROLLS out there!
YOU was supposed to get the ingredients!
NOBODY told me to!
I told you! Like a HUNDRED TIMES, I told you!
Sorry, I am no good at cooking but great at EATING!
CHIT-CHAT
CHIT-CHAT
CHIT-CHAT
CHIT-CHAT
CHIT-CHAT
We can't disappoint our guests--not like THIS!

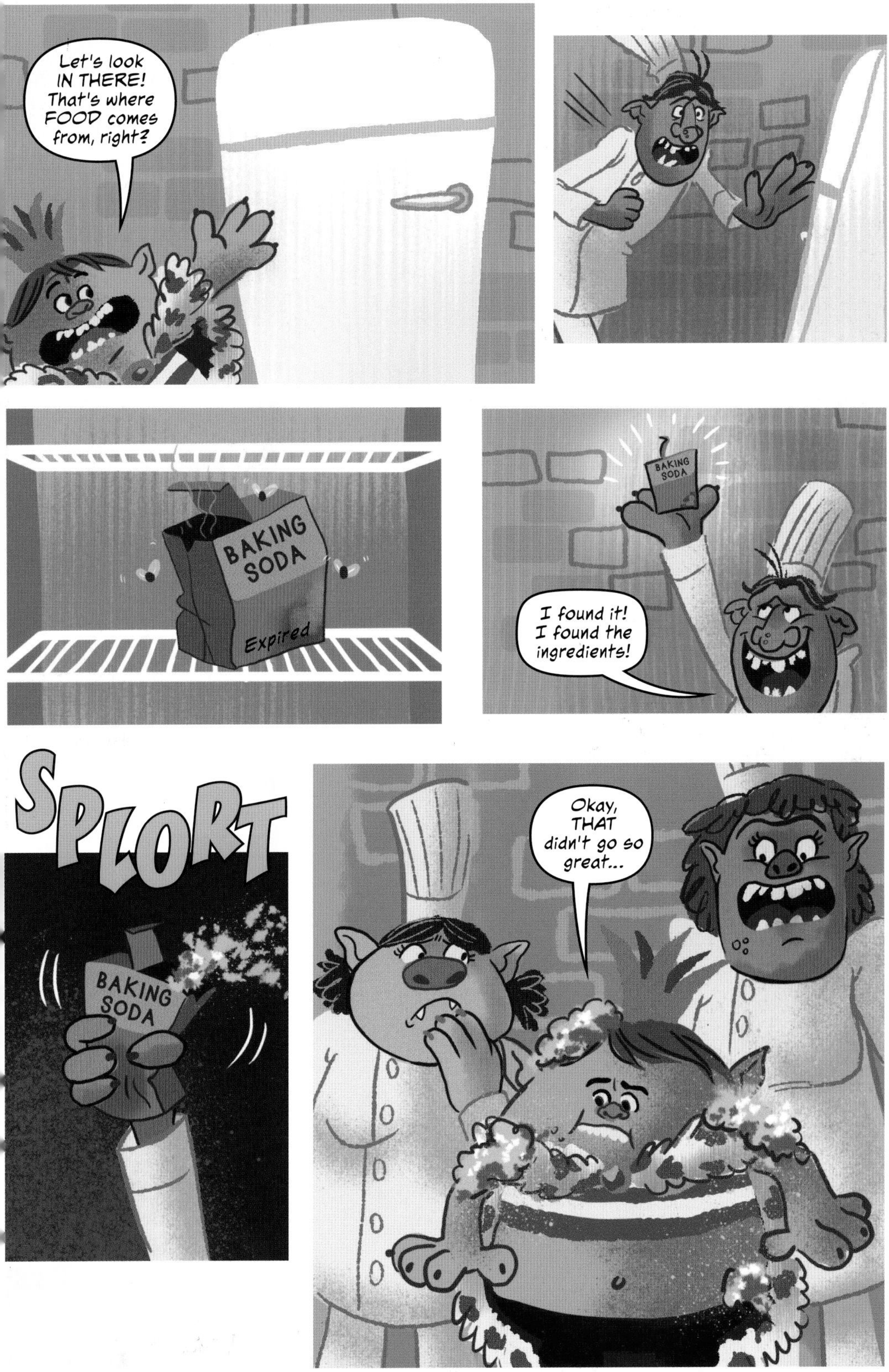
Let's look IN THERE! That's where FOOD comes from, right?
BAKING SODA
Expired
BAKING SODA
I found it! I found the ingredients!
SPLORT
BAKING SODA
Okay, THAT didn't go so great...

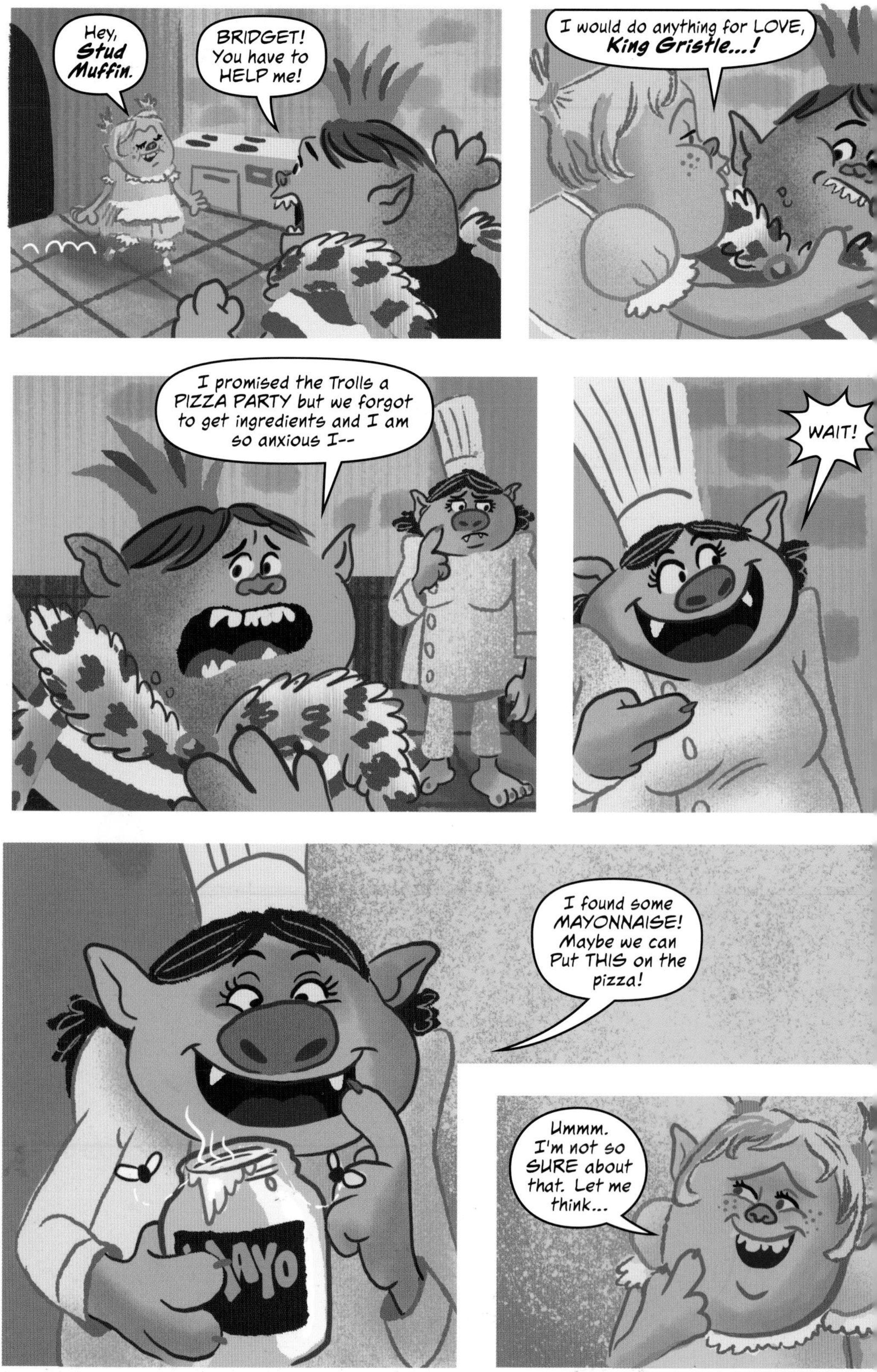
Hey, Stud Muffin.
BRIDGET! You have to HELP me!
I would do anything for LOVE, King Gristle...!
I promised the Trolls a PIZZA PARTY but we forgot to get ingredients and I am so anxious I--
WAIT!
I found some MAYONNAISE! Maybe we can Put THIS on the pizza!
MAYO
Ummm. I'm not so SURE about that. Let me think...

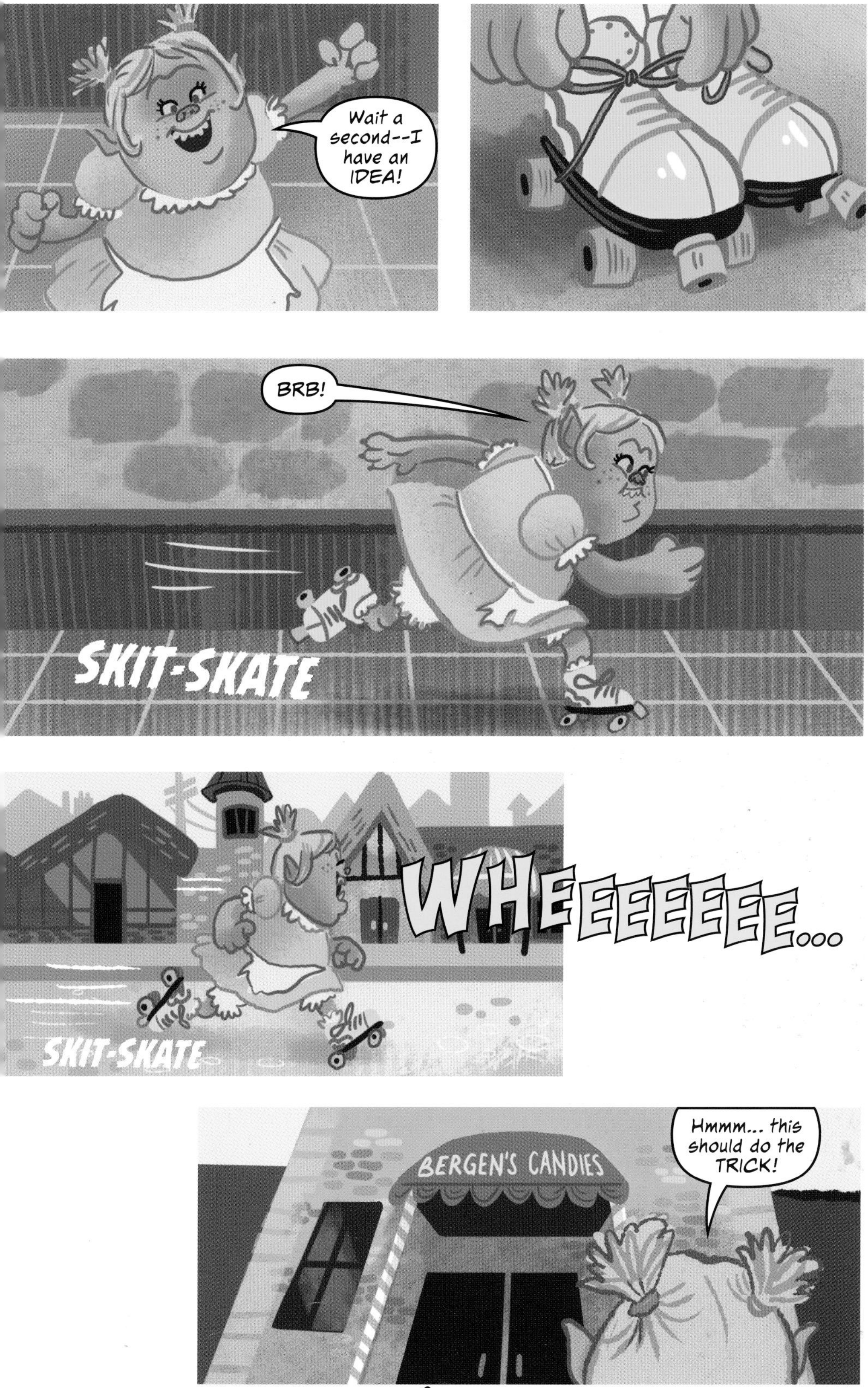
Wait a second--I have an IDEA!
BRB!
SKIT-SKATE
WHEEEEEEE...
SKIT-SKATE
BERGEN'S CANDIES
Hmmm... this should do the TRICK!

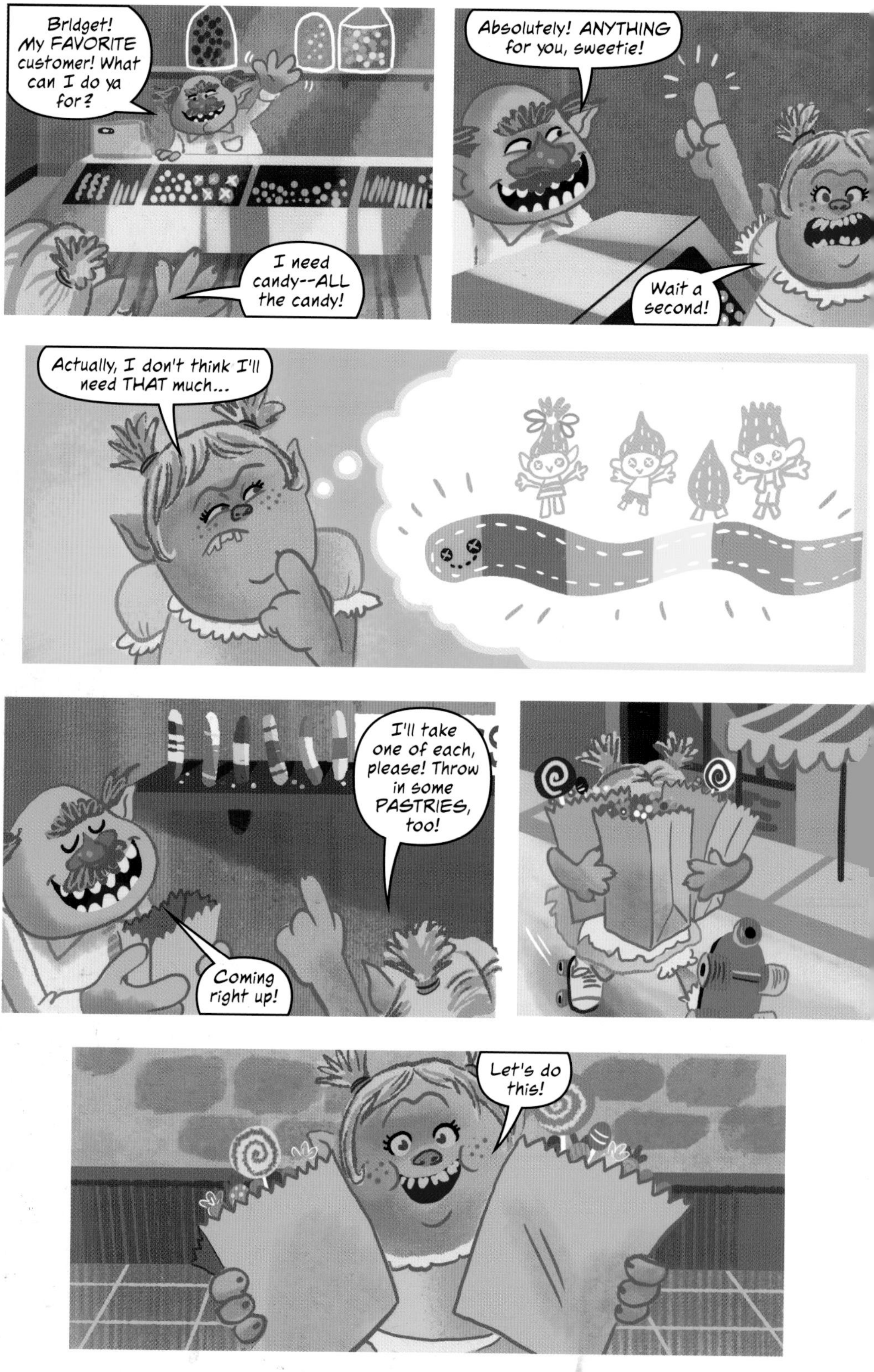
Bridget! My FAVORITE customer! What can I do ya for?
I need candy--ALL the candy!
Absolutely! ANYTHING for you, sweetie!
Wait a second!
Actually, I don't think I'll need THAT much...
I'll take one of each, please! Throw in some PASTRIES, too!
Coming right up!
Let's do this!

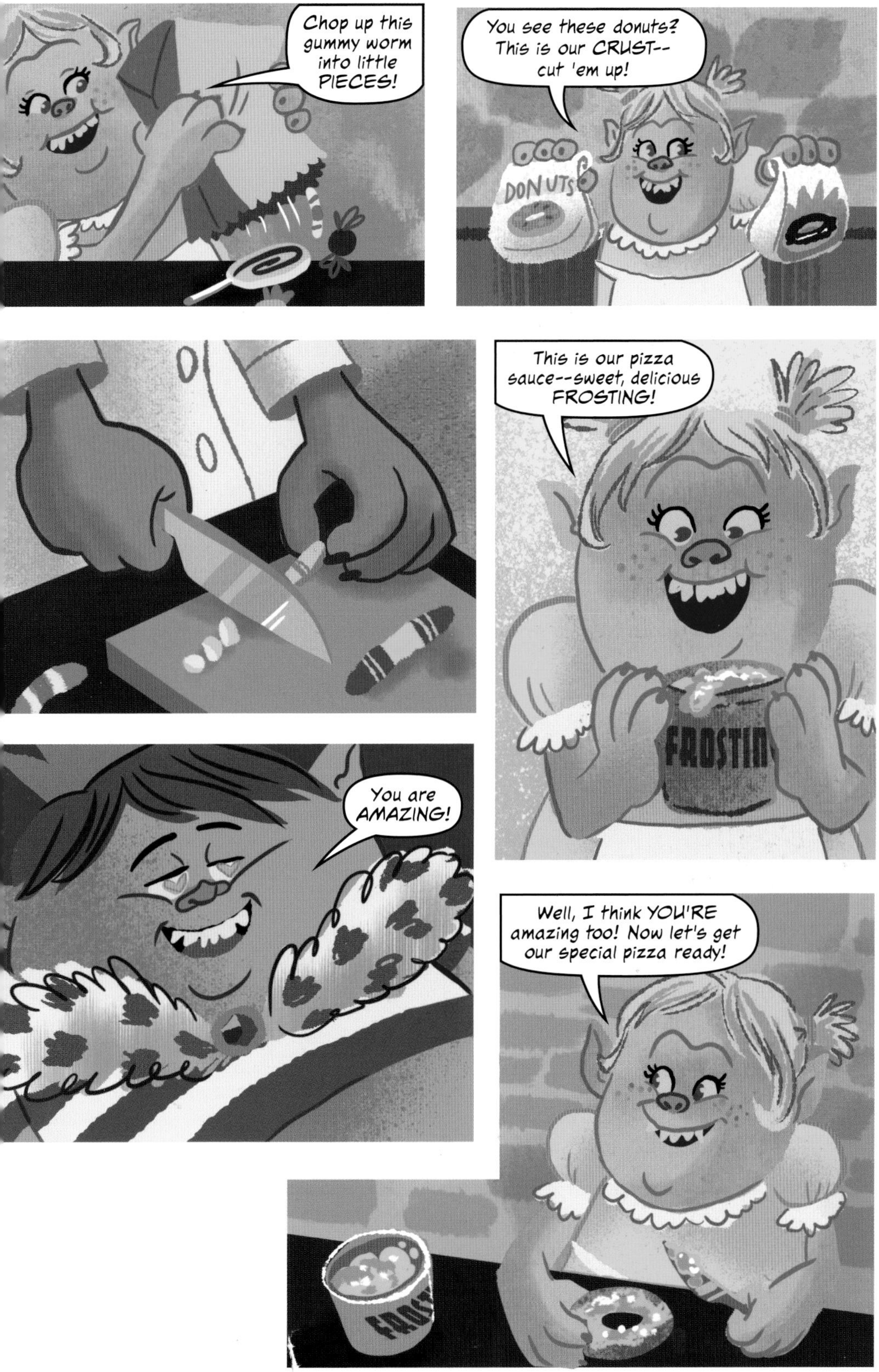
Chop up this gummy worm into little PIECES!
You see these donuts? This is our CRUST-- cut 'em up!
DONUTS
This is our pizza sauce--sweet, delicious FROSTING!
FROSTIN
You are AMAZING!
Well, I think YOU'RE amazing too! Now let's get our special pizza ready!

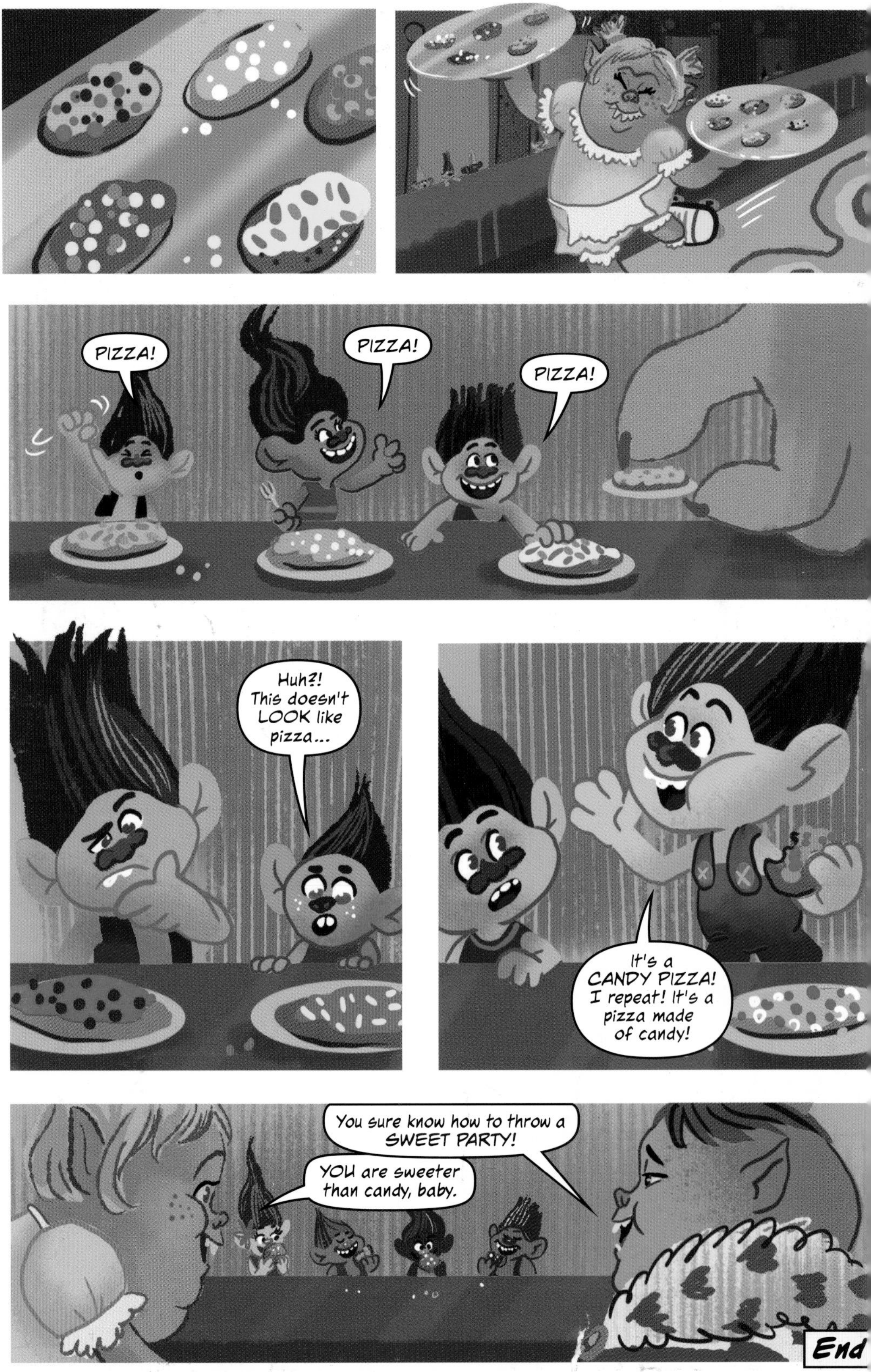
PIZZA!
PIZZA!
PIZZA!
Huh?! This doesn't LOOK like pizza...
It's a CANDY PIZZA! I repeat! It's a pizza made of candy!
You sure know how to throw a SWEET PARTY!
YOU are sweeter than candy, baby.
End

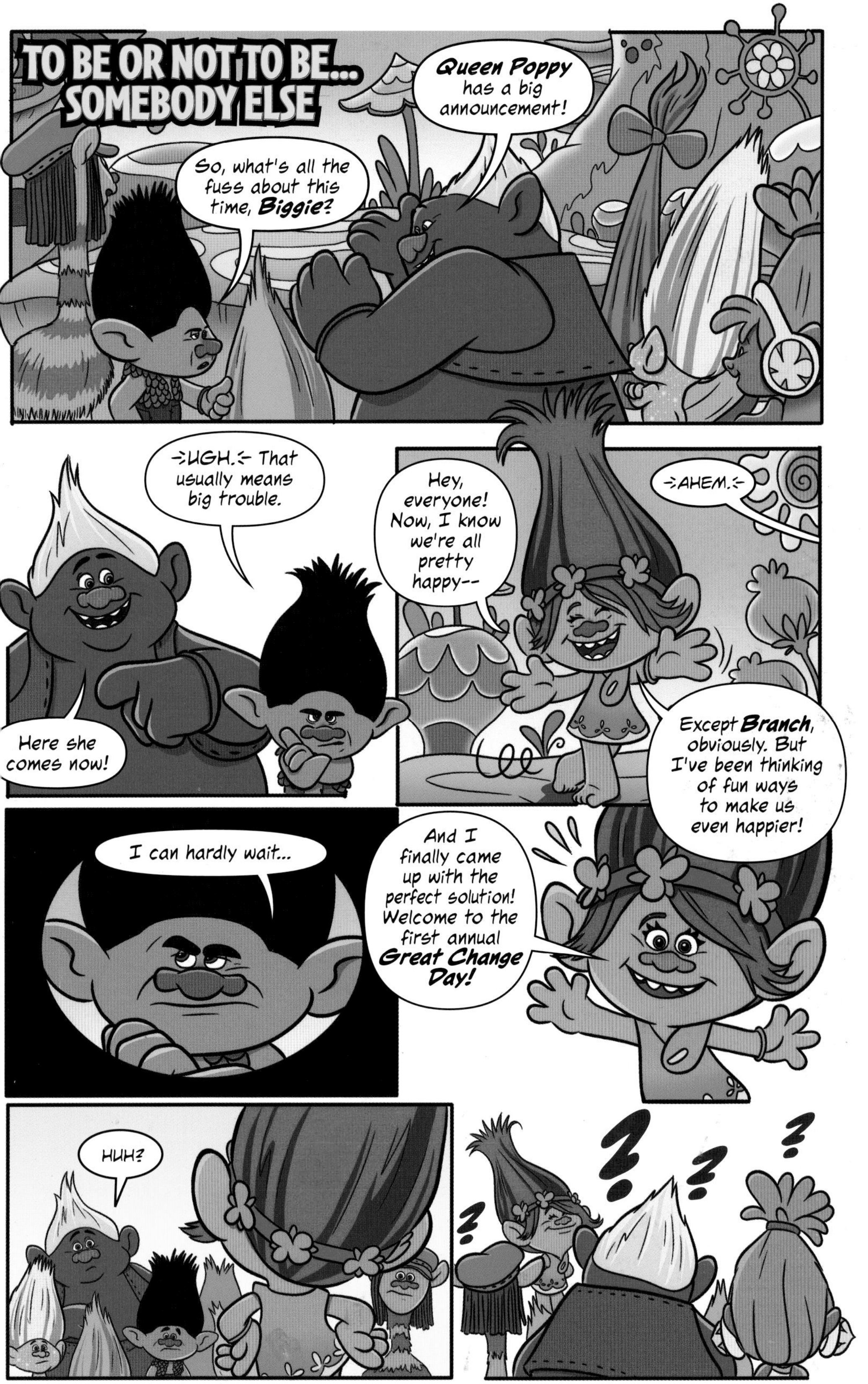
TO BE OR NOT TO BE... SOMEBODY ELSE
So, what's all the fuss about this time, Biggie?
Queen Poppy has a big announcement!
UGH. That usually means big trouble.
Here she comes now!
AHEM.
Hey, everyone! Now, I know we're all pretty happy--
Except Branch, obviously. But I've been thinking of fun ways to make us even happier!
I can hardly wait...
And I finally came up with the perfect solution! Welcome to the first annual Great Change Day!
HUH?

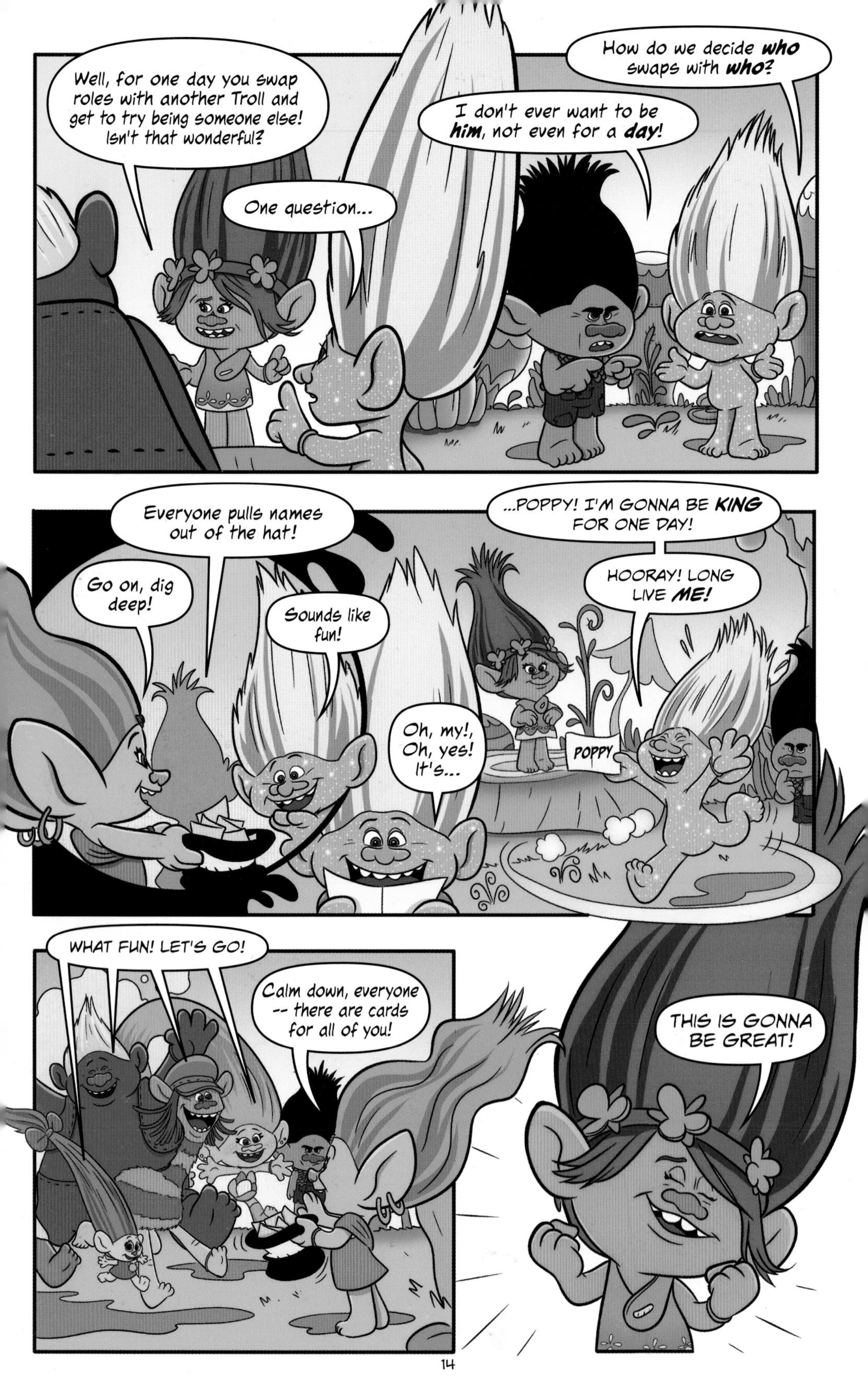
Well, for one day you swap roles with another Troll and get to try being someone else! Isn't that wonderful?
One question...
I don't ever want to be him, not even for a day!
How do we decide who swaps with who?
Everyone pulls names out of the hat!
Go on, dig deep!
Sounds like fun!
Oh, my!, Oh, yes! It's...
...POPPY! I'M GONNA BE KING FOR ONE DAY!
POPPY
HOORAY! LONG LIVE ME!
WHAT FUN! LET'S GO!
Calm down, everyone -- there are cards for all of you!
THIS IS GONNA BE GREAT!

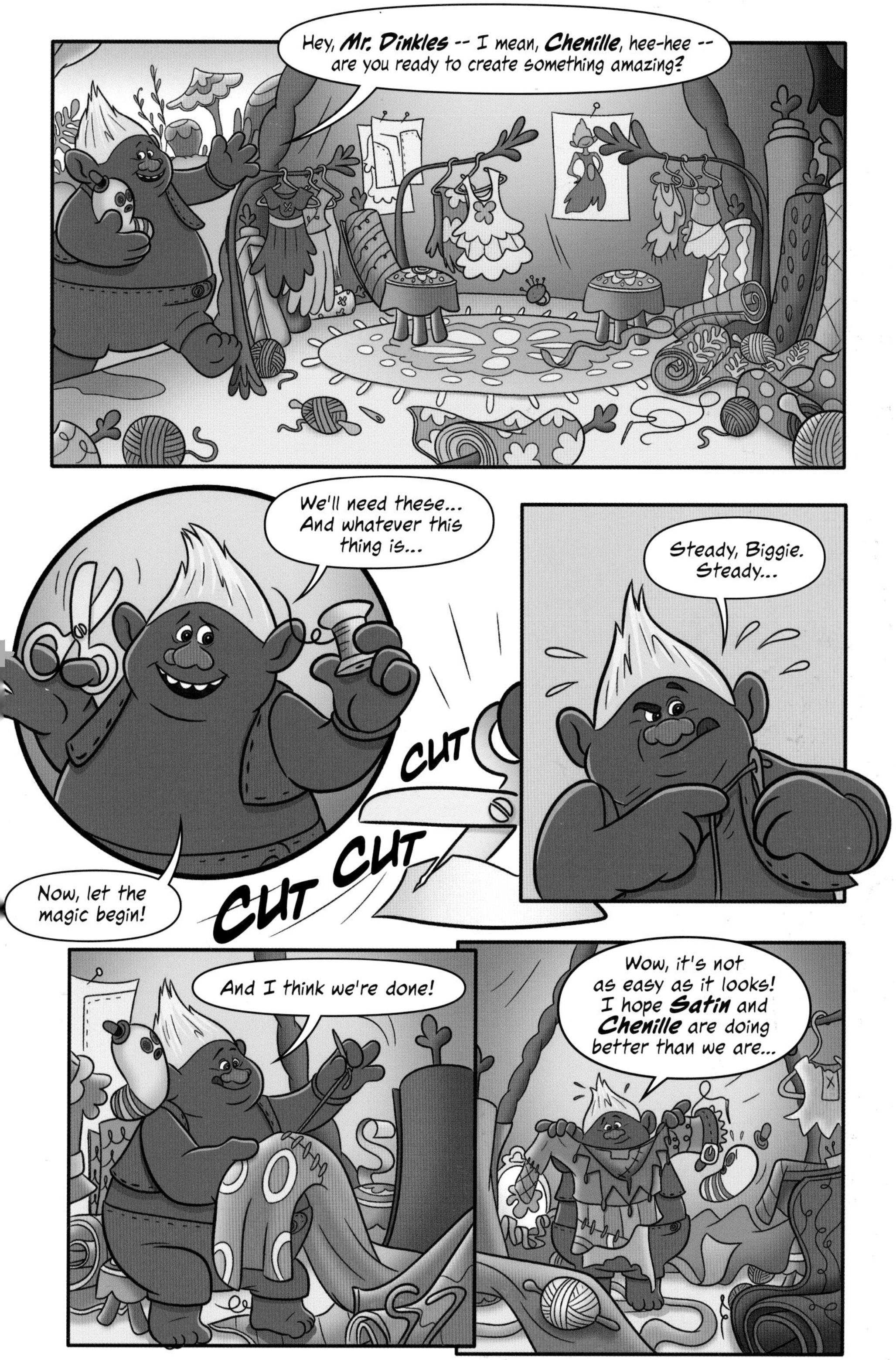
Hey, **Mr. Dinkles** -- I mean, **Chenille**, hee-hee -- are you ready to create something amazing?
We'll need these... And whatever this thing is...
Now, let the magic begin!
CUT
CUT CUT
Steady, Biggie. Steady...
And I think we're done!
Wow, it's not as easy as it looks! I hope **Satin** and **Chenille** are doing better than we are...

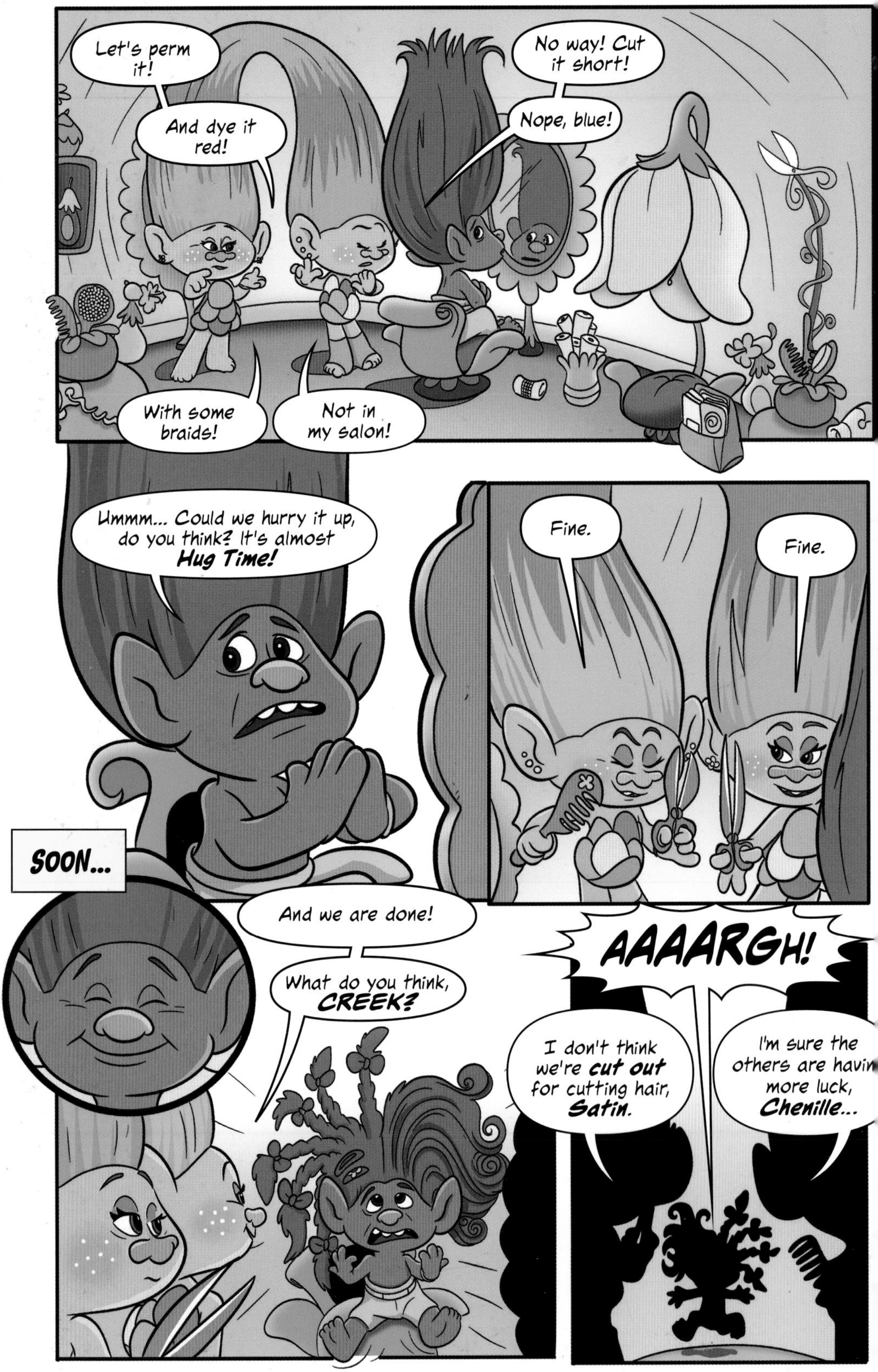

Let's perm it!
And dye it red!
No way! Cut it short!
Nope, blue!
With some braids!
Not in my salon!
Ummm... Could we hurry it up, do you think? It's almost **Hug Time!**
Fine.
Fine.
SOON...
And we are done!
What do you think, **CREEK?**
AAAARGH!
I don't think we're ***cut out*** for cutting hair, ***Satin***.
I'm sure the others are havin more luck, ***Chenille...***

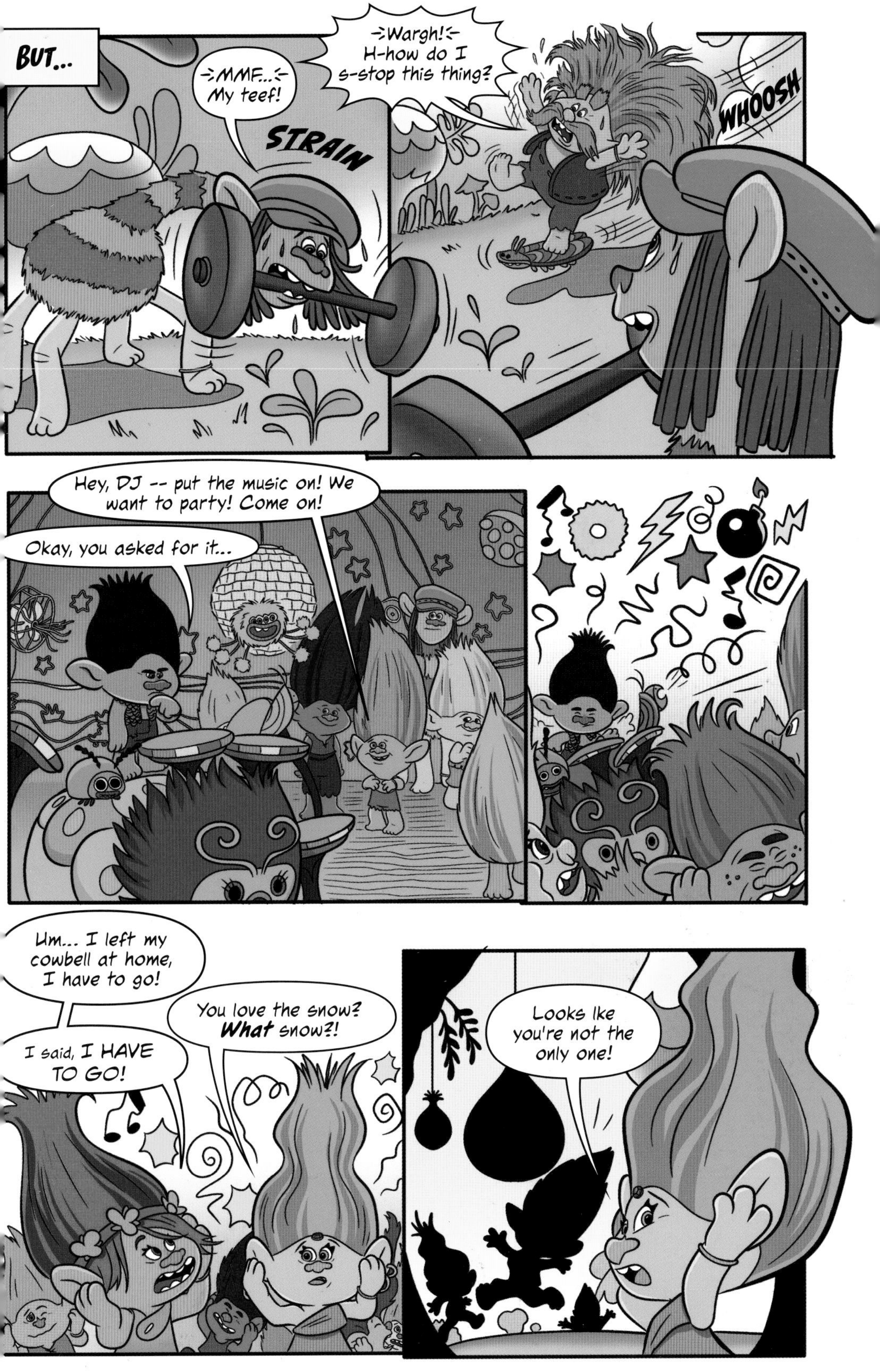
BUT...
MMF... My teef!
STRAIN
Wargh! H-how do I s-stop this thing?
WHOOSH
Hey, DJ -- put the music on! We want to party! Come on!
Okay, you asked for it...
Um... I left my cowbell at home, I have to go!
I said, I HAVE TO GO!
You love the snow? *What* snow?!
Looks lke you're not the only one!

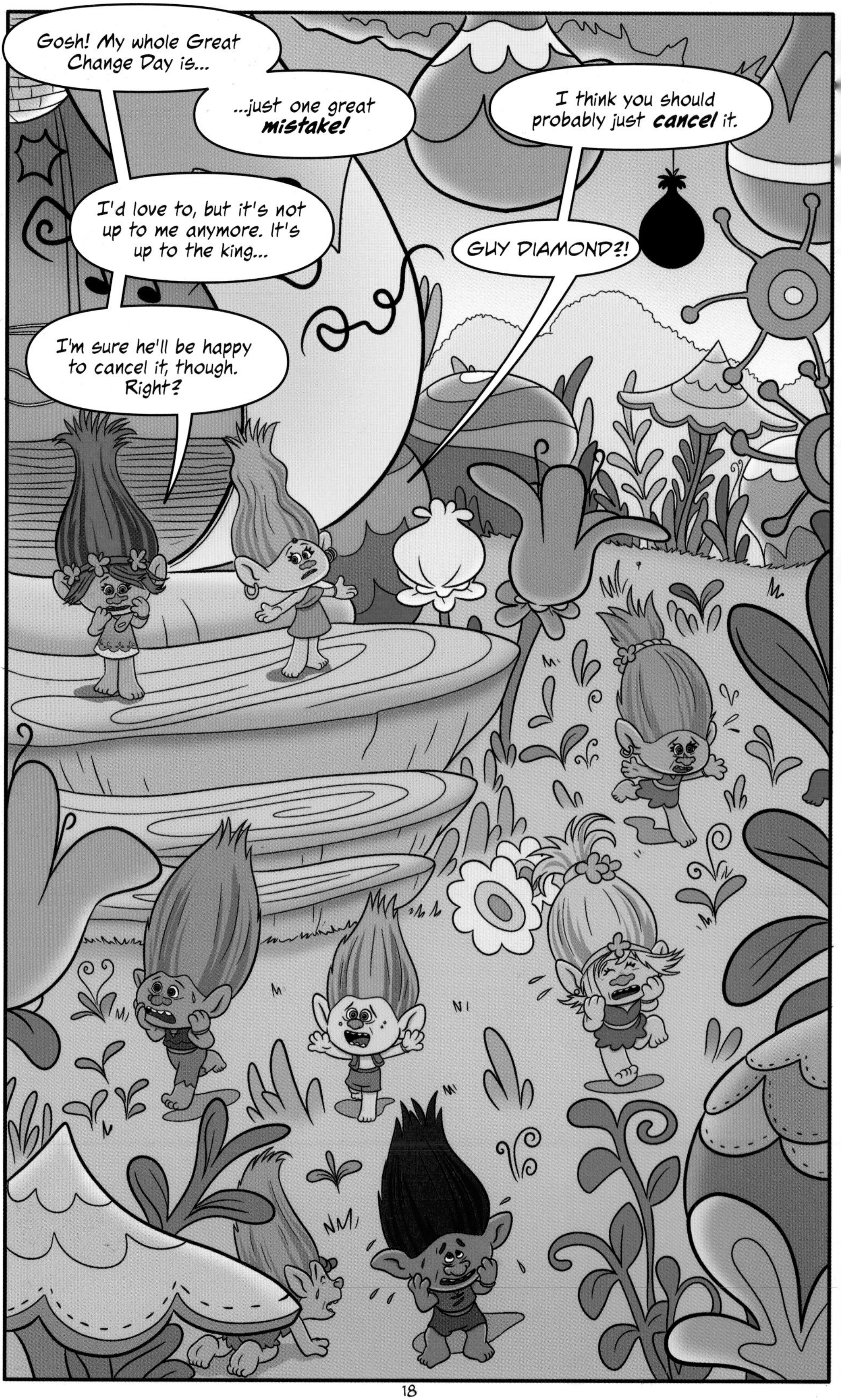
Gosh! My whole Great Change Day is...
...just one great **mistake!**
I think you should probably just **cancel** it.
I'd love to, but it's not up to me anymore. It's up to the king...
GUY DIAMOND?!
I'm sure he'll be happy to cancel it, though. Right?

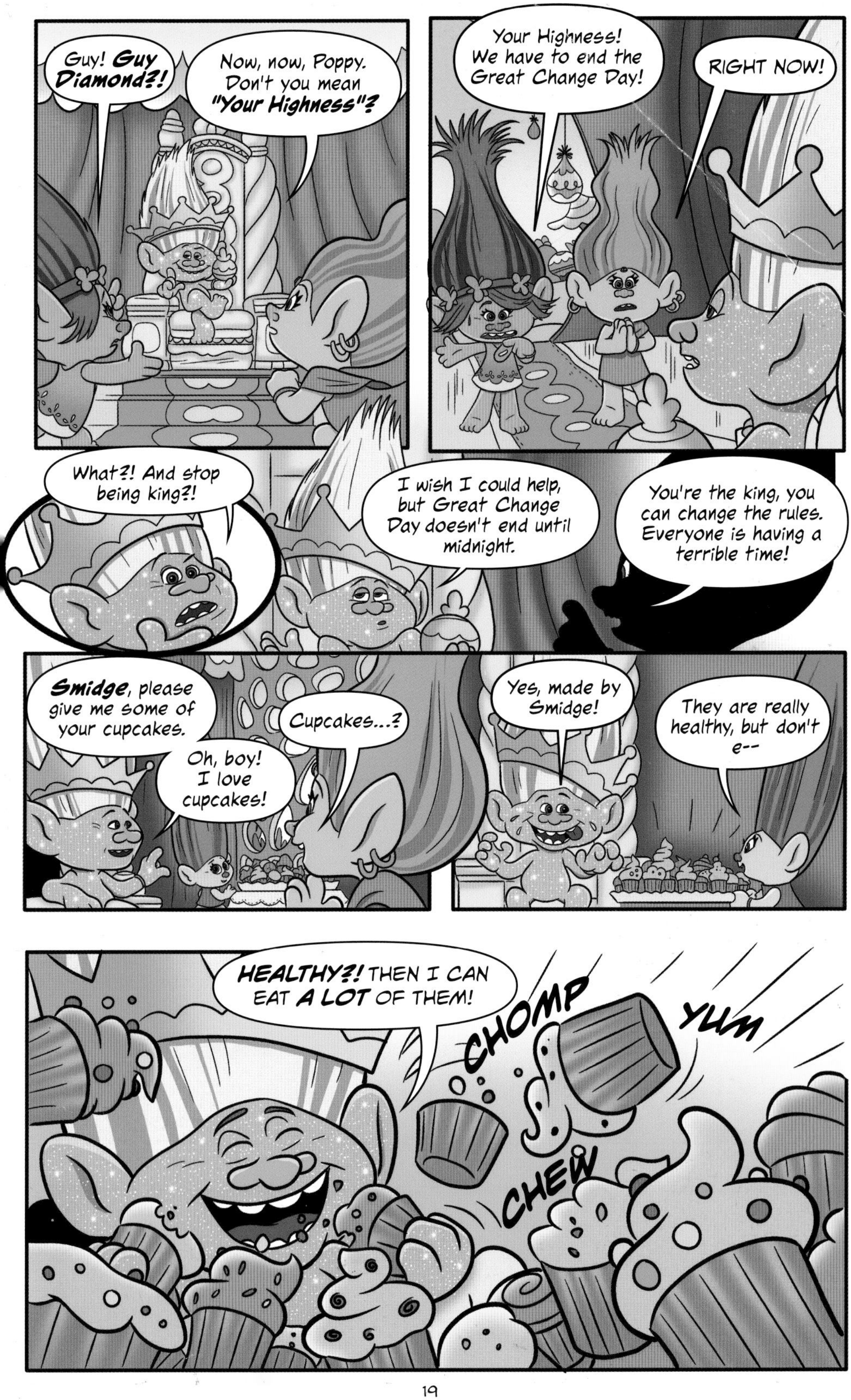
Guy! **Guy Diamond?!**
Now, now, Poppy. Don't you mean **"Your Highness"?**
Your Highness! We have to end the Great Change Day!
RIGHT NOW!
What?! And stop being king?!
I wish I could help, but Great Change Day doesn't end until midnight.
You're the king, you can change the rules. Everyone is having a terrible time!
Smidge, please give me some of your cupcakes.
Oh, boy! I love cupcakes!
Cupcakes...?
Yes, made by Smidge!
They are really healthy, but don't e--
HEALTHY?! THEN I CAN EAT **A LOT** OF THEM!
CHOMP
YUM
CHEW

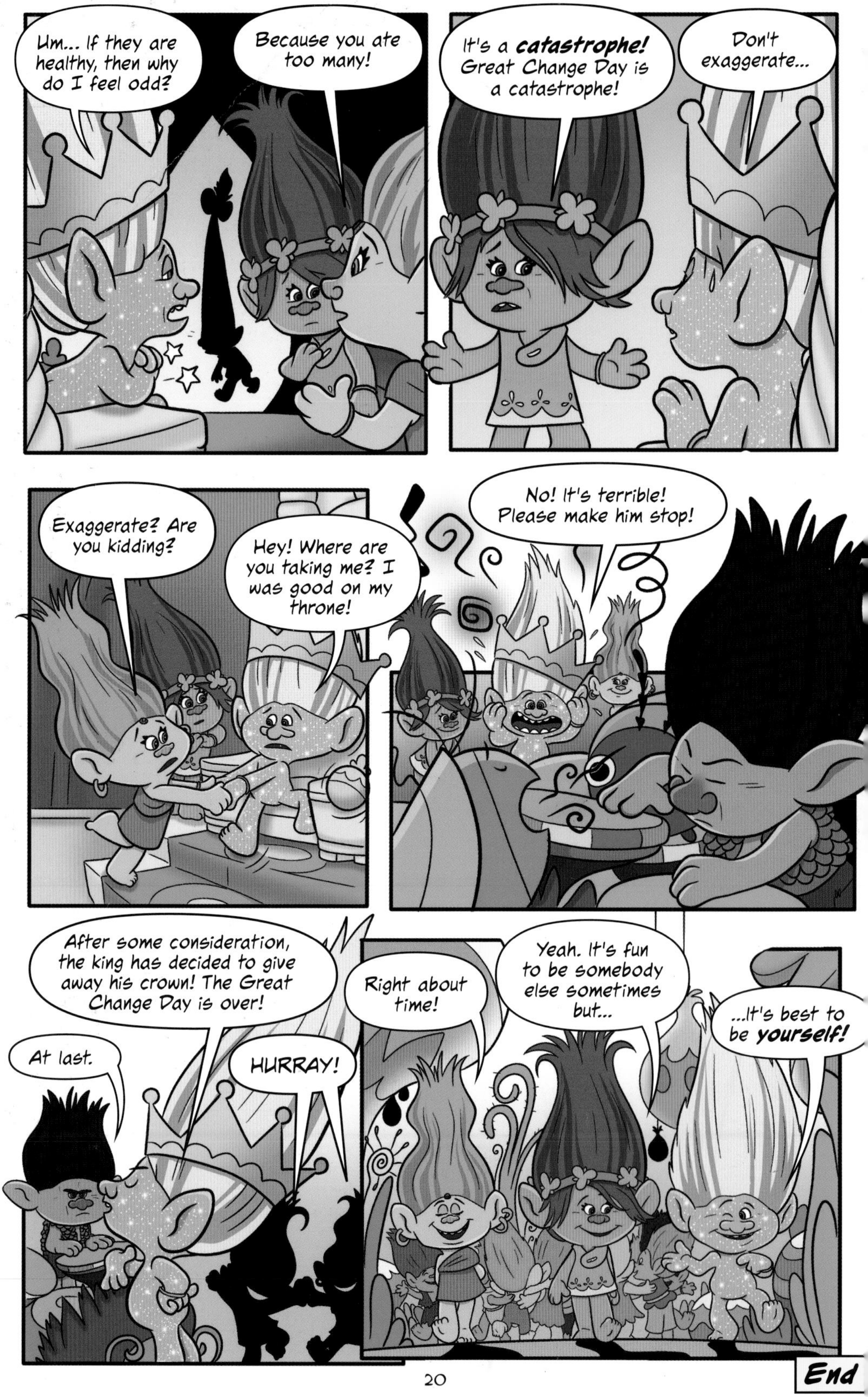
Um... If they are healthy, then why do I feel odd?
Because you ate too many!
It's a **catastrophe!** Great Change Day is a catastrophe!
Don't exaggerate...
Exaggerate? Are you kidding?
Hey! Where are you taking me? I was good on my throne!
No! It's terrible! Please make him stop!
After some consideration, the king has decided to give away his crown! The Great Change Day is over!
At last.
HURRAY!
Right about time!
Yeah. It's fun to be somebody else sometimes but...
...It's best to be **yourself!**
End

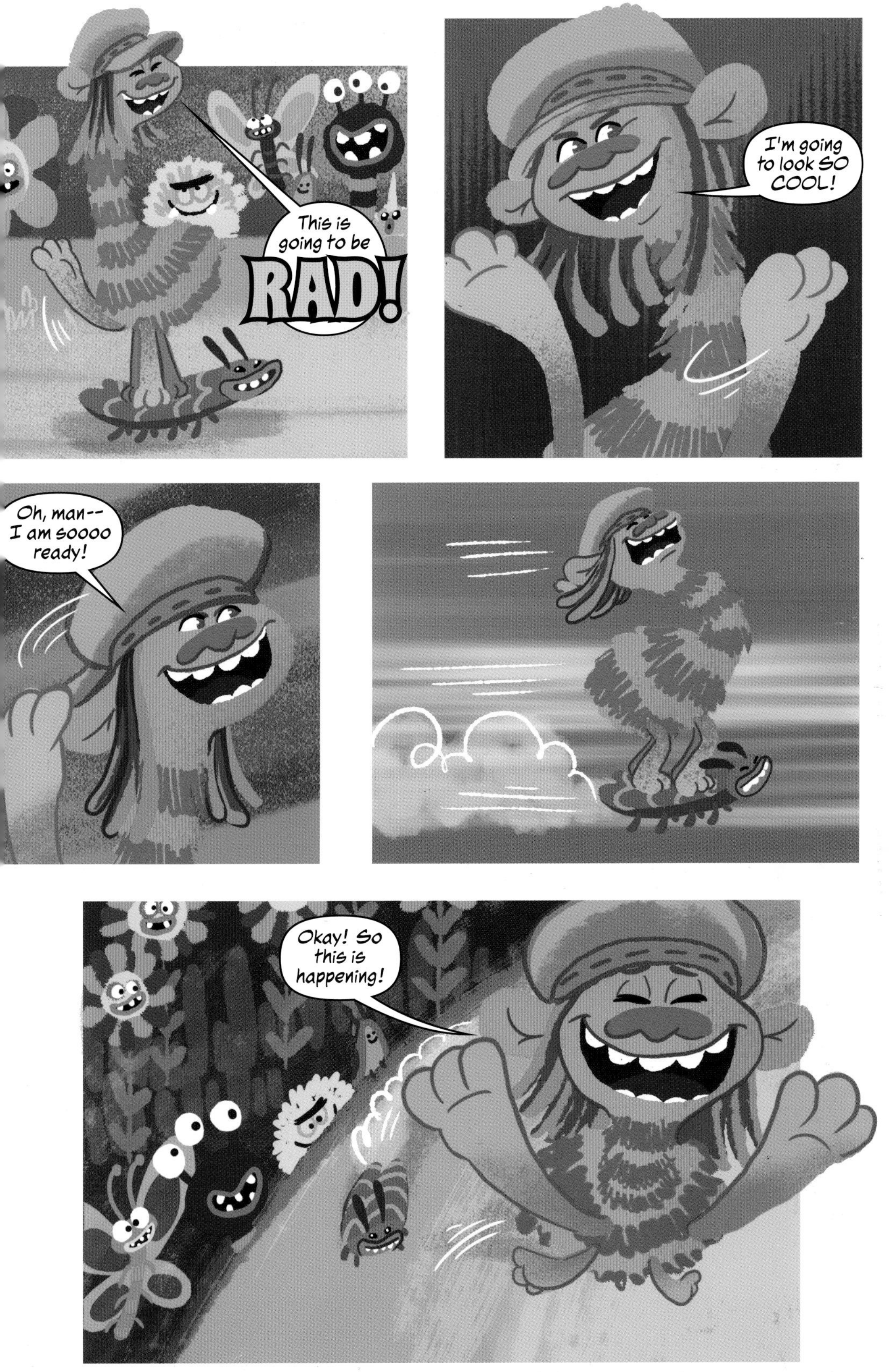

This is going to be RAD!
I'm going to look SO COOL!
Oh, man-- I am soooo ready!
Okay! So this is happening!

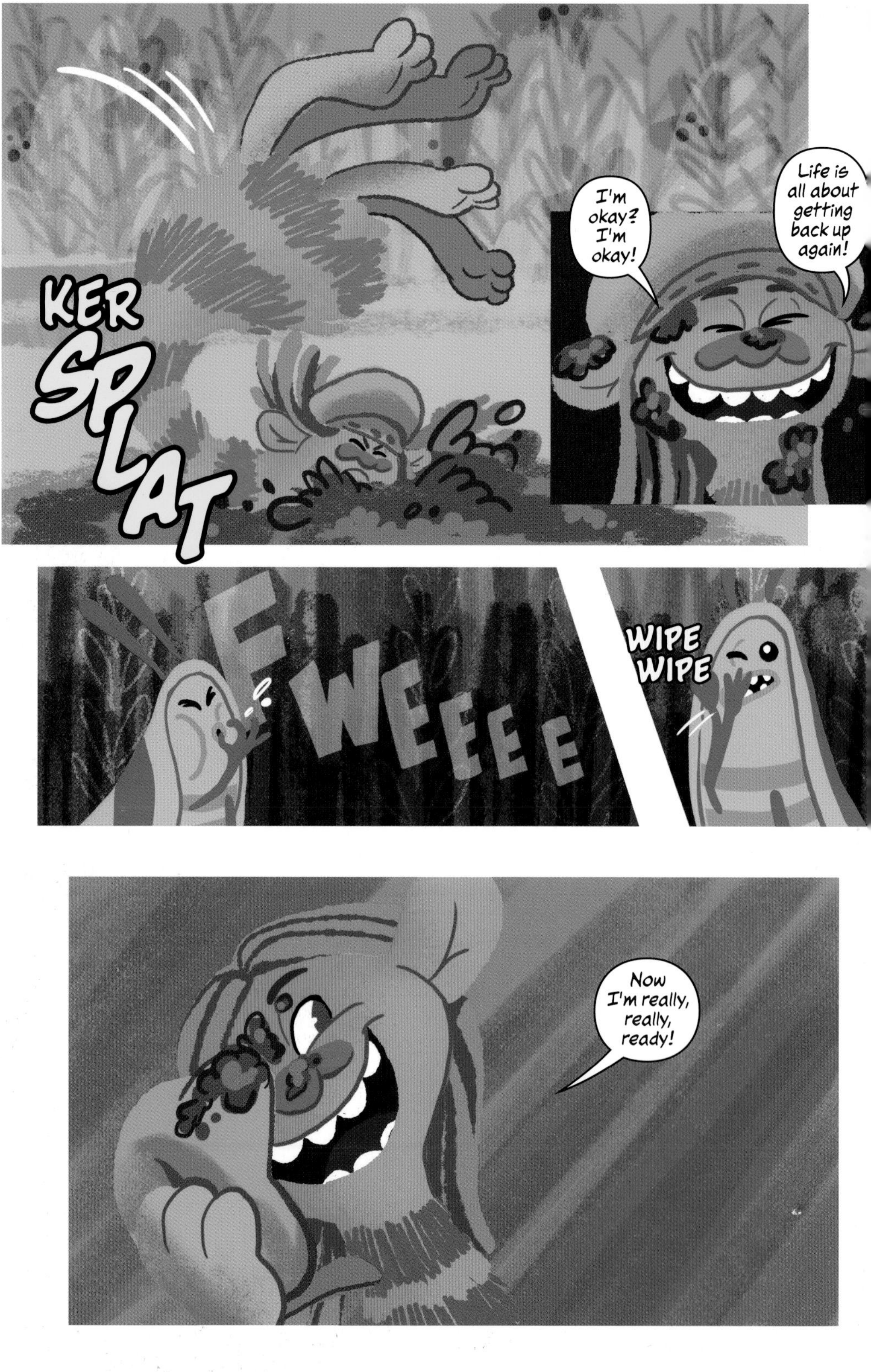
KER SPLAT
I'm okay? I'm okay!
Life is all about getting back up again!
FWEEEE
WIPE WIPE
Now I'm really, really, ready!

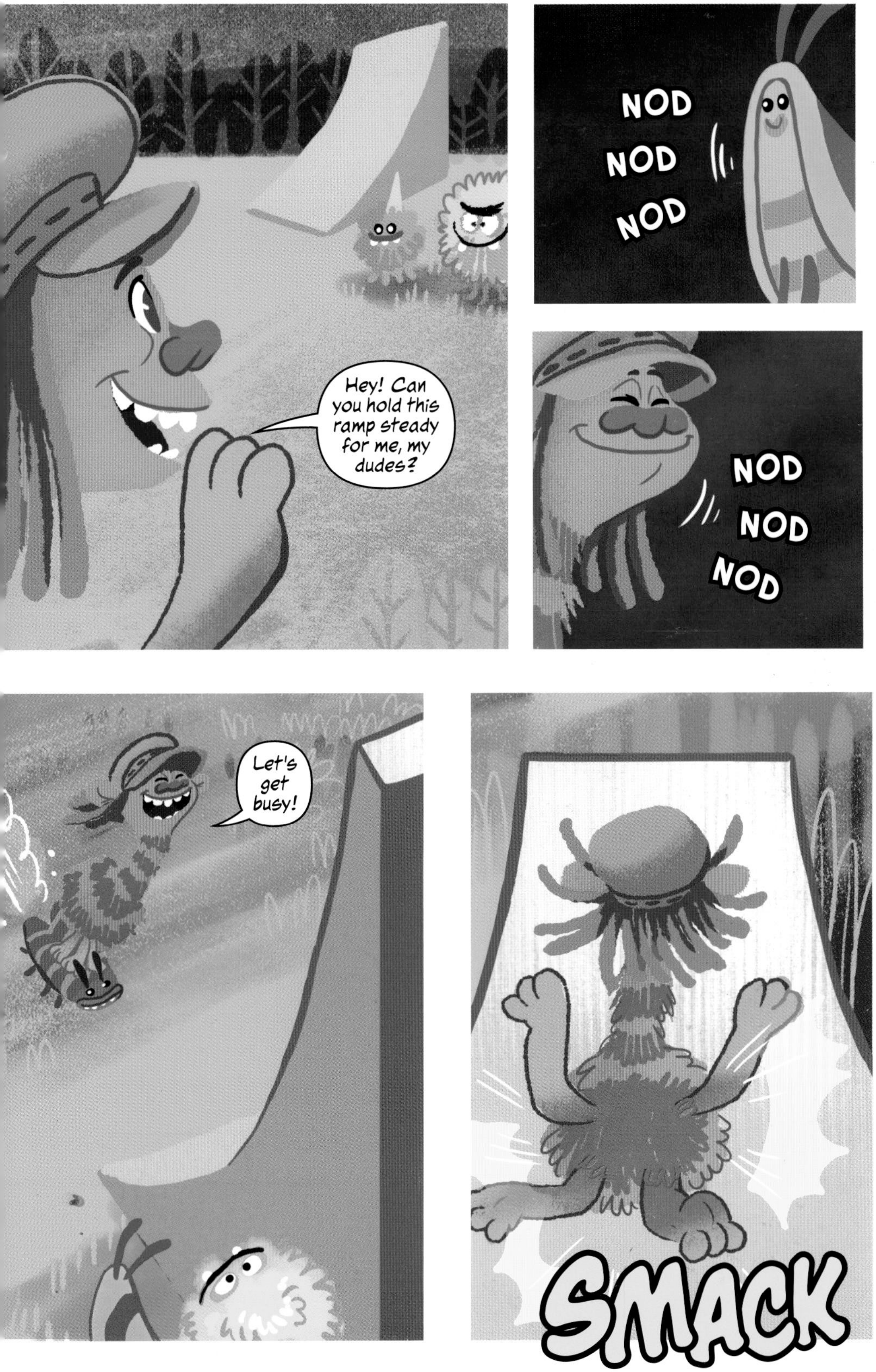
Hey! Can you hold this ramp steady for me, my dudes?
NOD
NOD
NOD
NOD
NOD
NOD
Let's get busy!
SMACK

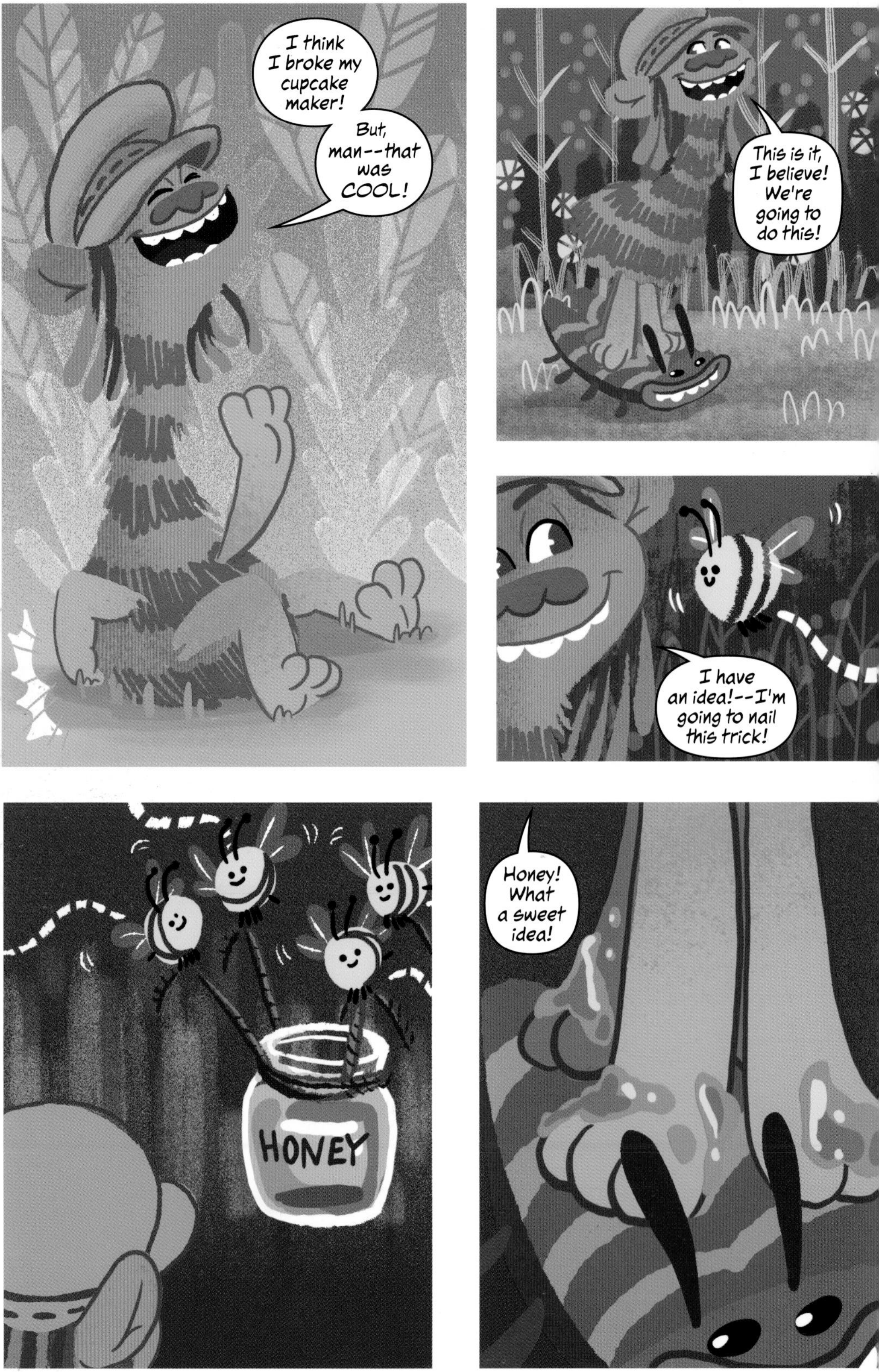
I think I broke my cupcake maker!
But, man--that was COOL!
This is it, I believe! We're going to do this!
I have an idea!--I'm going to nail this trick!
HONEY
Honey! What a sweet idea!

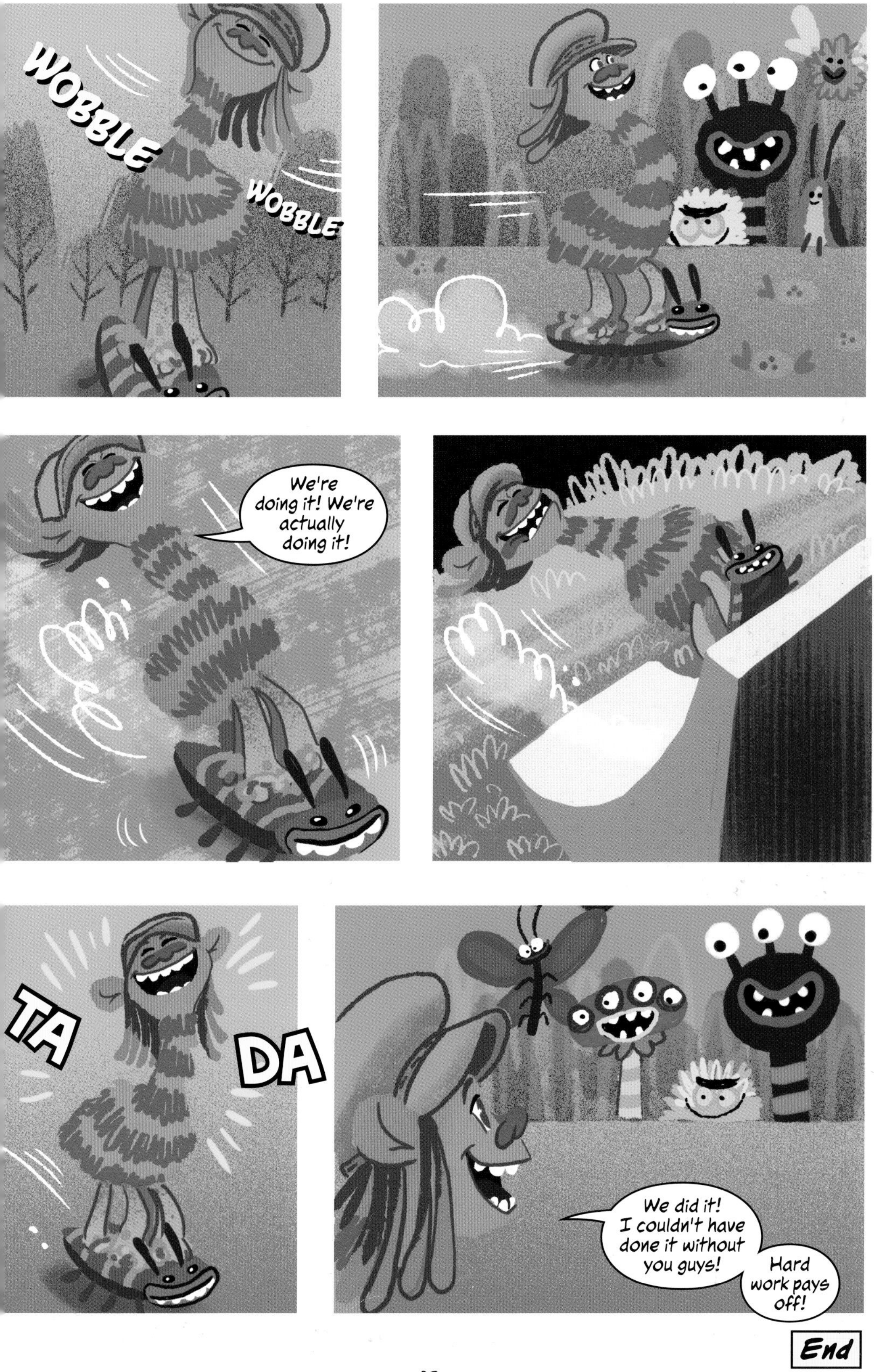
WOBBLE
WOBBLE
We're doing it! We're actually doing it!
TA
DA
We did it! I couldn't have done it without you guys!
Hard work pays off!
End

ROYAL PORTRAIT

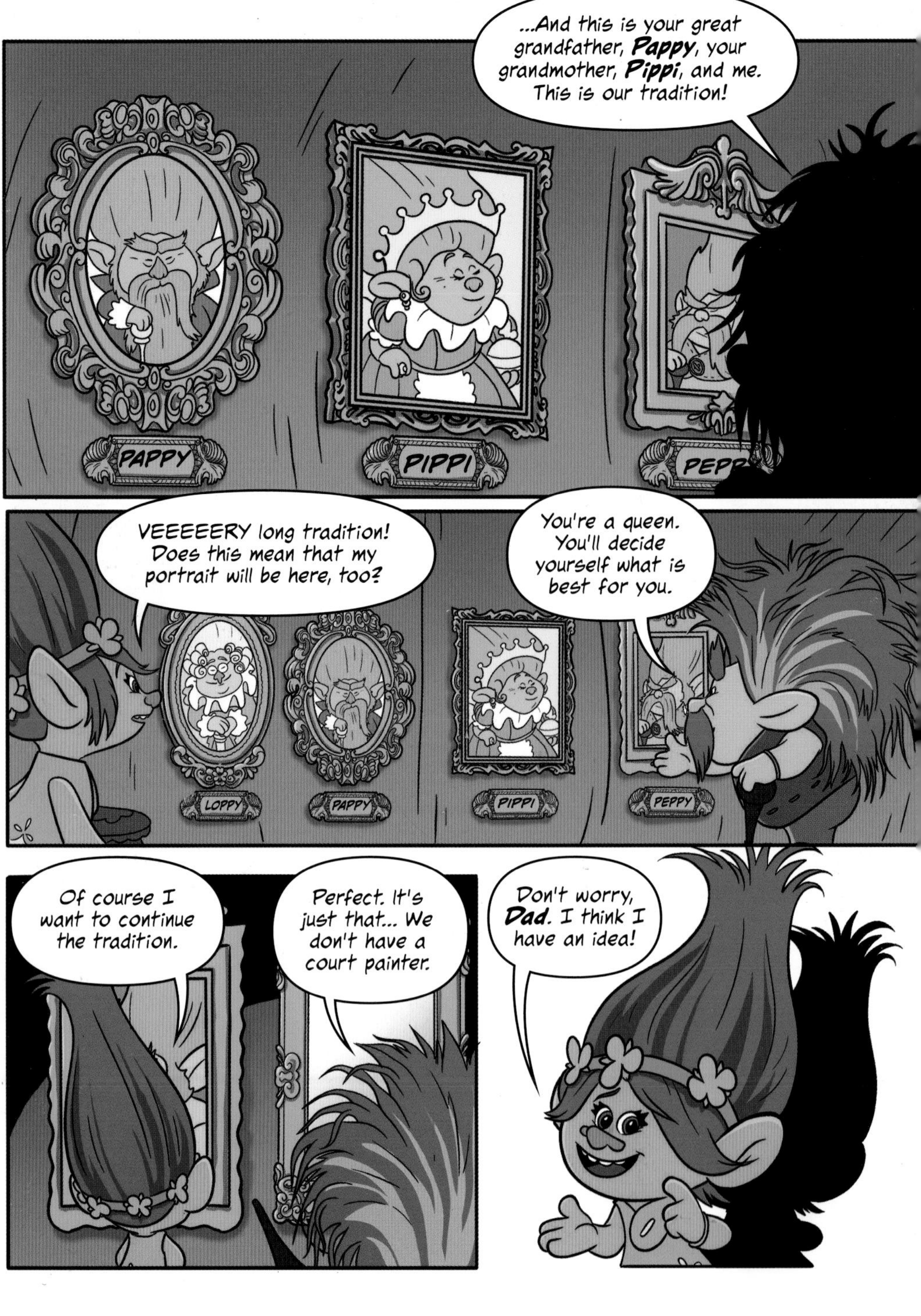

...And this is your great grandfather, Pappy, your grandmother, Pippi, and me. This is our tradition!
PAPPY
PIPPI
VEEEEERY long tradition! Does this mean that my portrait will be here, too?
You're a queen. You'll decide yourself what is best for you.
LOPPY
PAPPY
PIPPI
PEPPY
Of course I want to continue the tradition.
Perfect. It's just that... We don't have a court painter.
Don't worry, Dad. I think I have an idea!

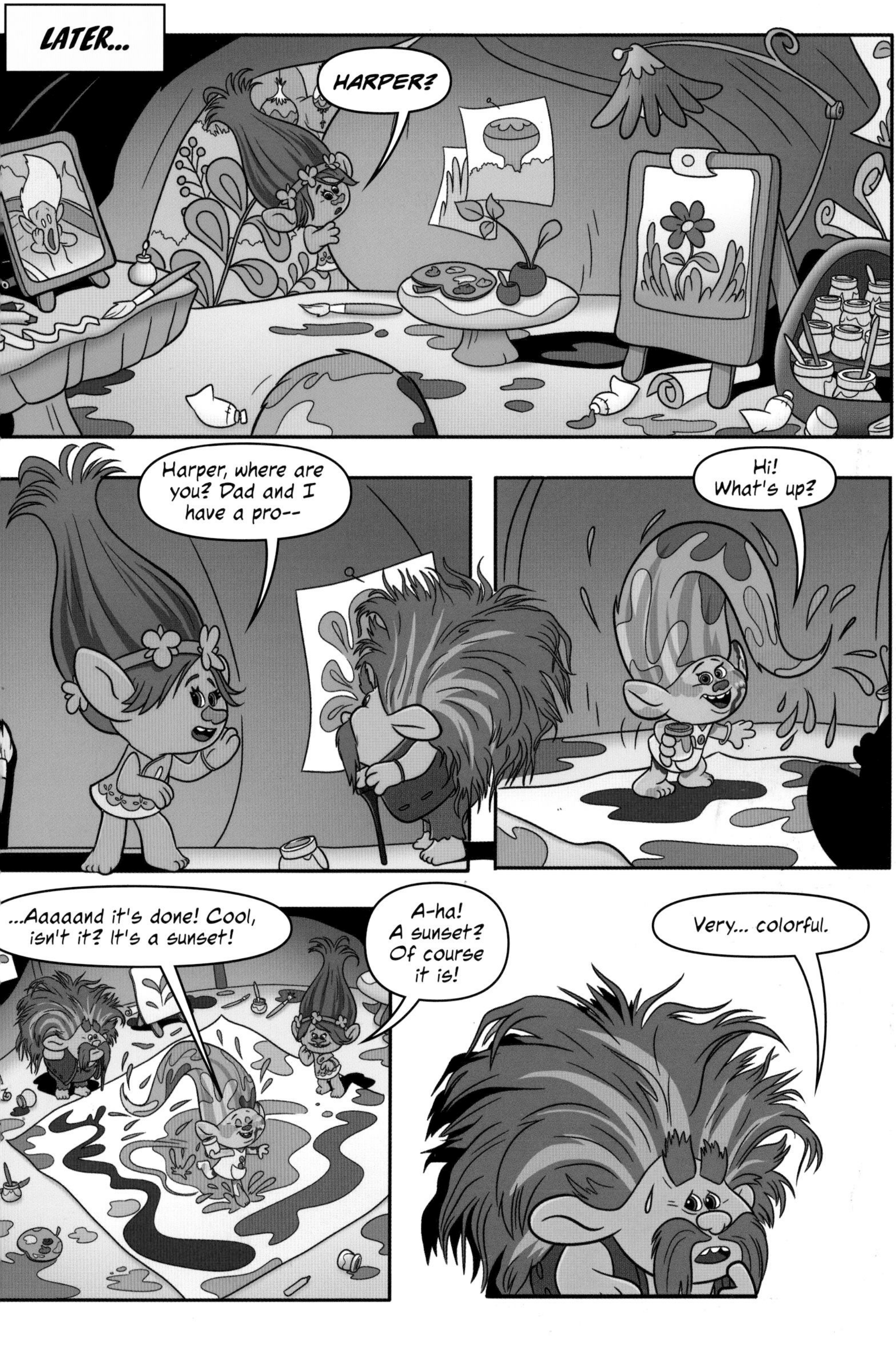
LATER...
HARPER?
Harper, where are you? Dad and I have a pro--
Hi! What's up?
...Aaaaand it's done! Cool, isn't it? It's a sunset!
A-ha! A sunset? Of course it is!
Very... colorful.

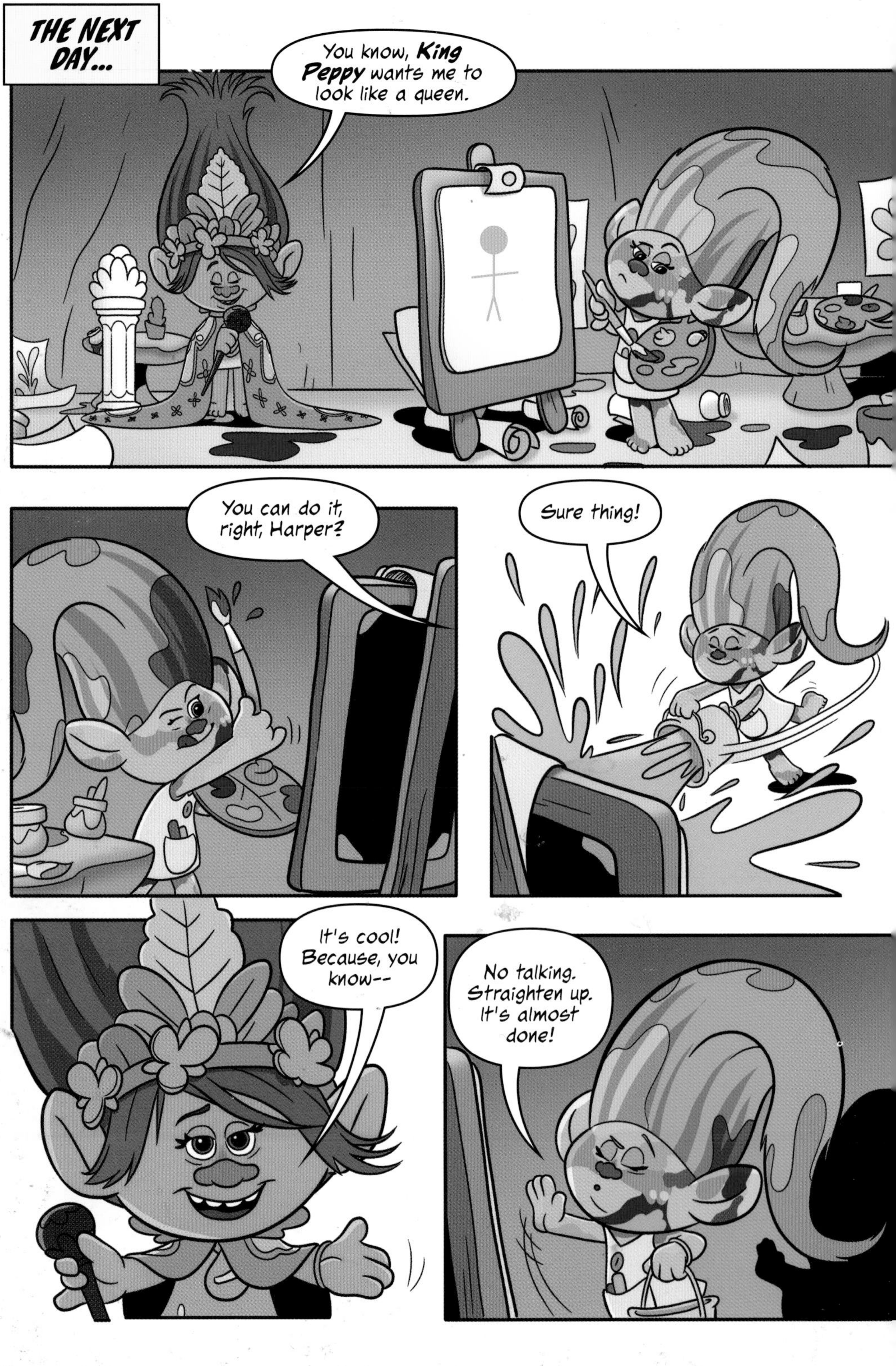
THE NEXT DAY...
You know, King Peppy wants me to look like a queen.
You can do it, right, Harper?
Sure thing!
It's cool! Because, you know--
No talking. Straighten up. It's almost done!

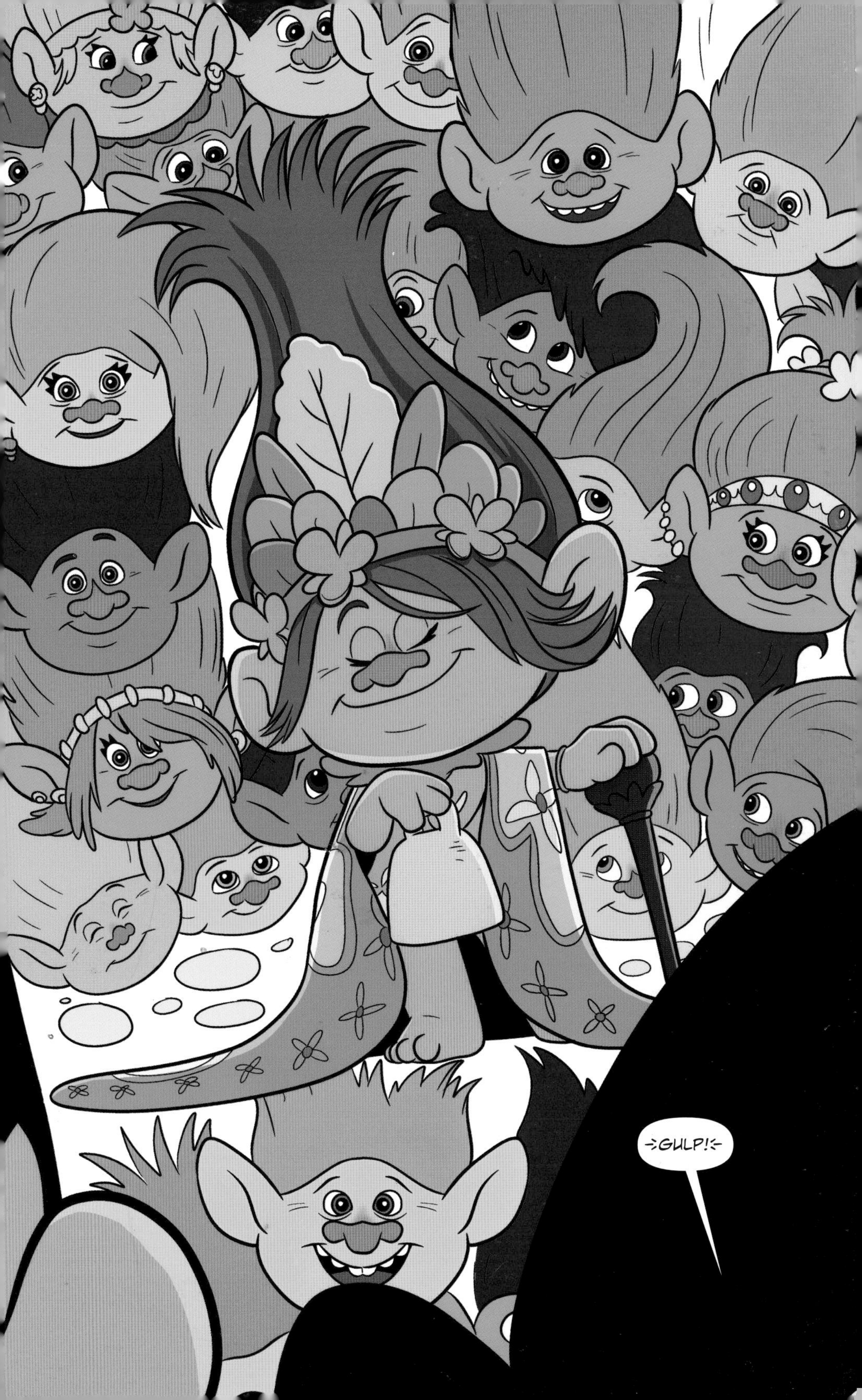
GULP!

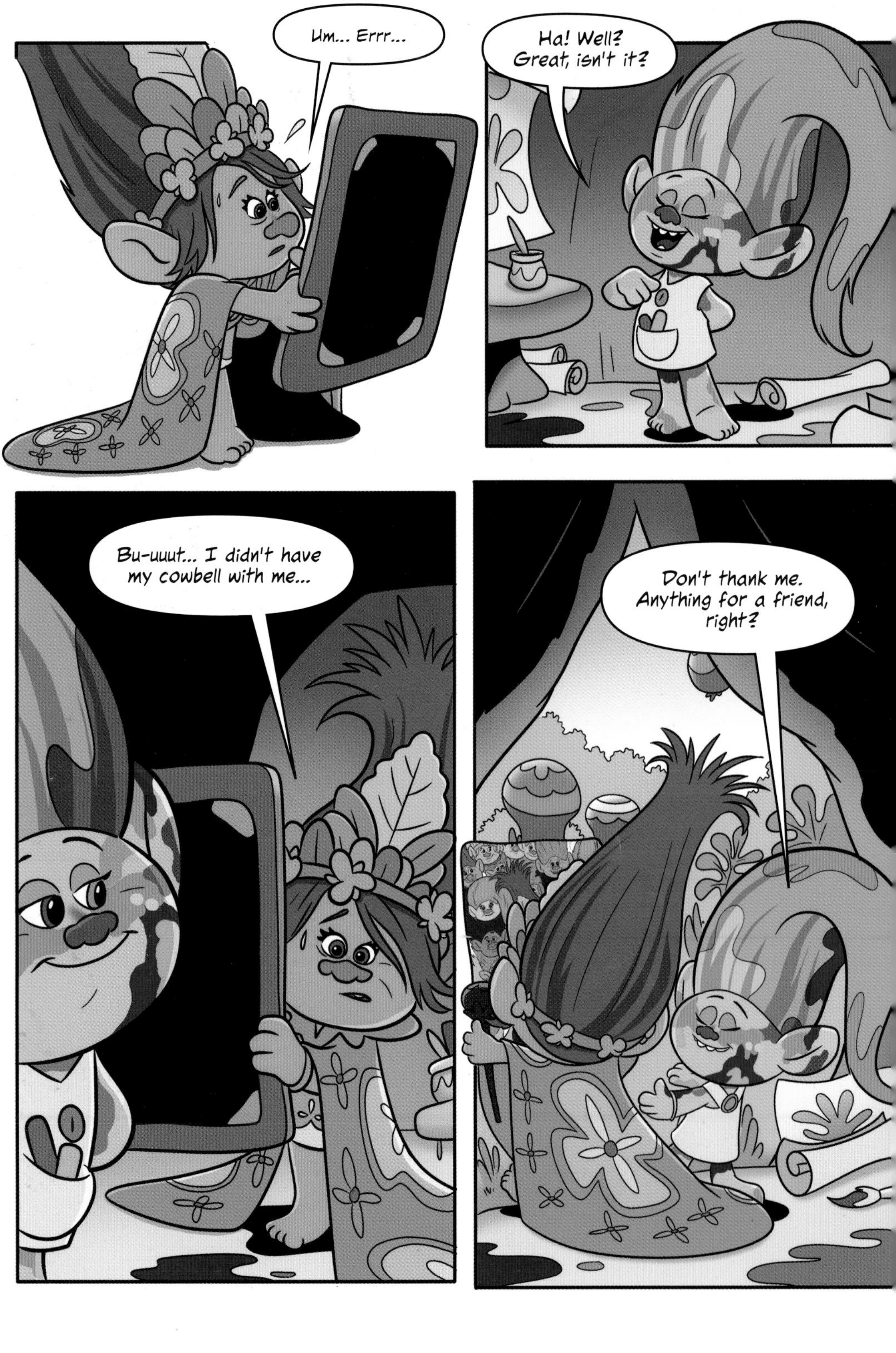
Um... Errr...
Ha! Well? Great, isn't it?
Bu-uuut... I didn't have my cowbell with me...
Don't thank me. Anything for a friend, right?

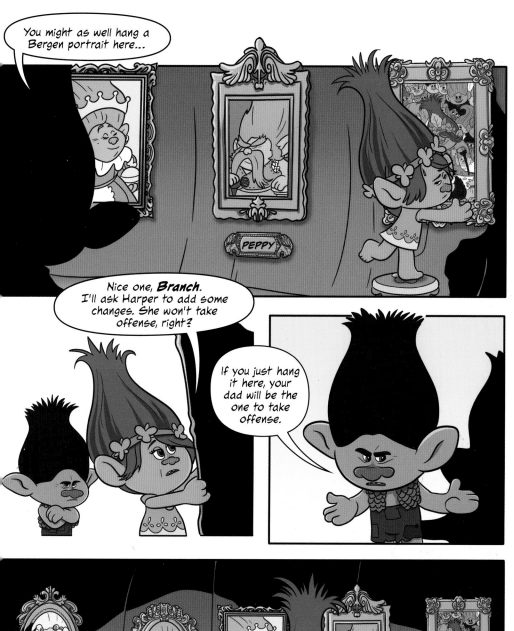

You might as well hang a Bergen portrait here...

PEPPY

Nice one, **Branch.** I'll ask Harper to add some changes. She won't take offense, right?

If you just hang it here, your dad will be the one to take offense.

PAPPY

PEPPY

You'll see. It'll be fine.

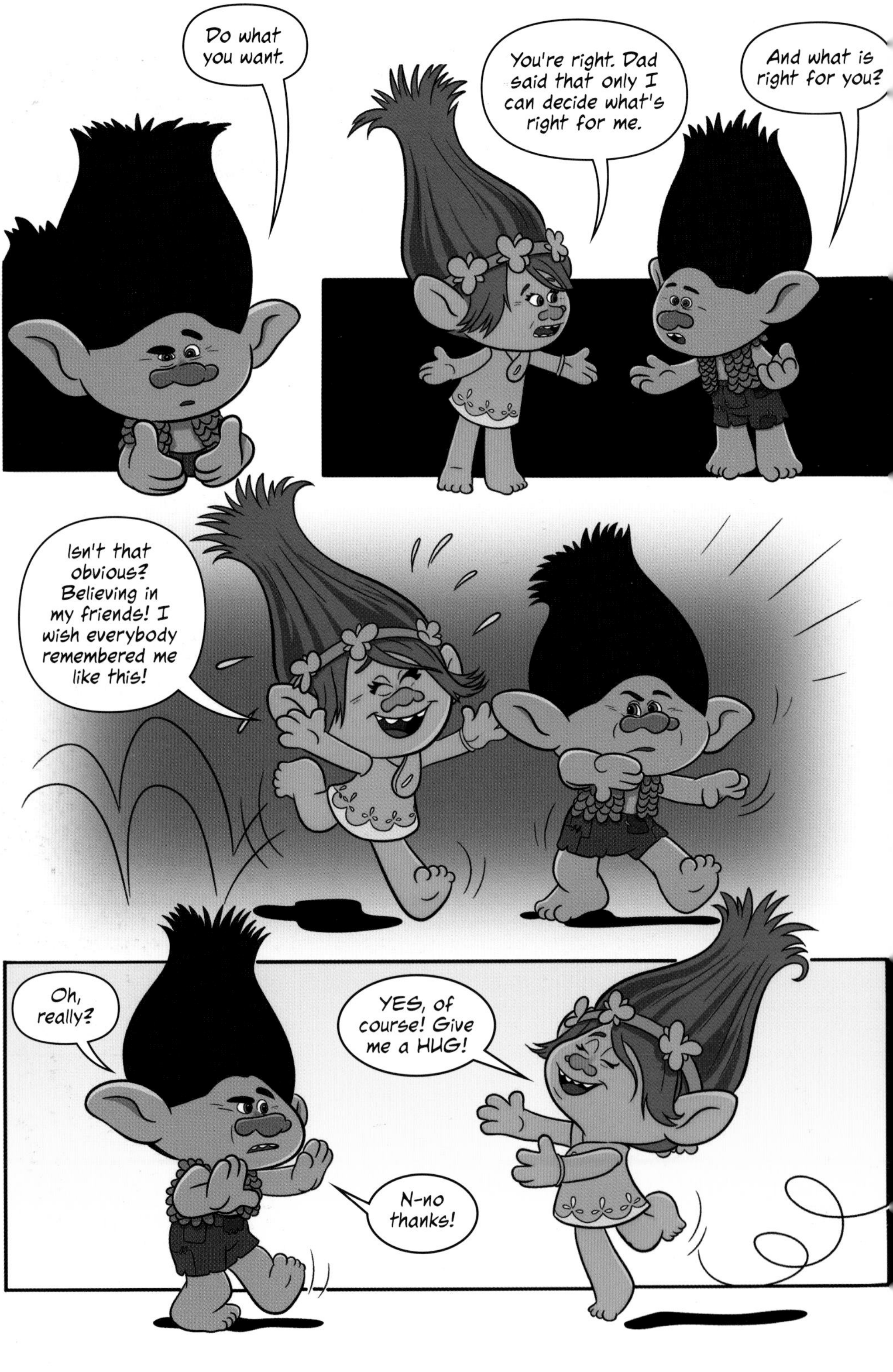
Do what you want.
You're right. Dad said that only I can decide what's right for me.
And what is right for you?
Isn't that obvious? Believing in my friends! I wish everybody remembered me like this!
Oh, really?
YES, of course! Give me a HUG!
N-no thanks!

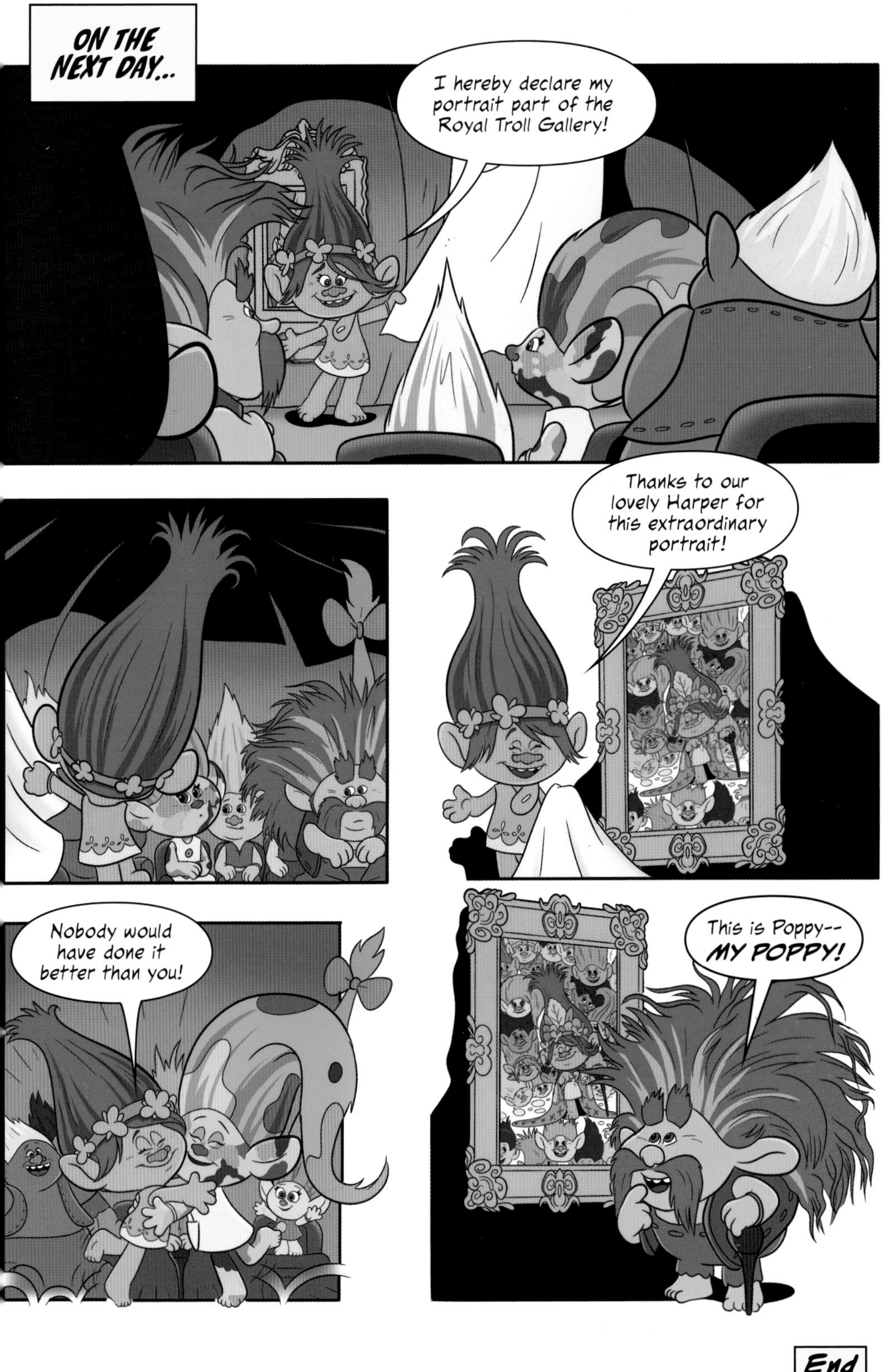

ON THE NEXT DAY...
I hereby declare my portrait part of the Royal Troll Gallery!
Thanks to our lovely Harper for this extraordinary portrait!
Nobody would have done it better than you!
This is Poppy-- MY POPPY!
End

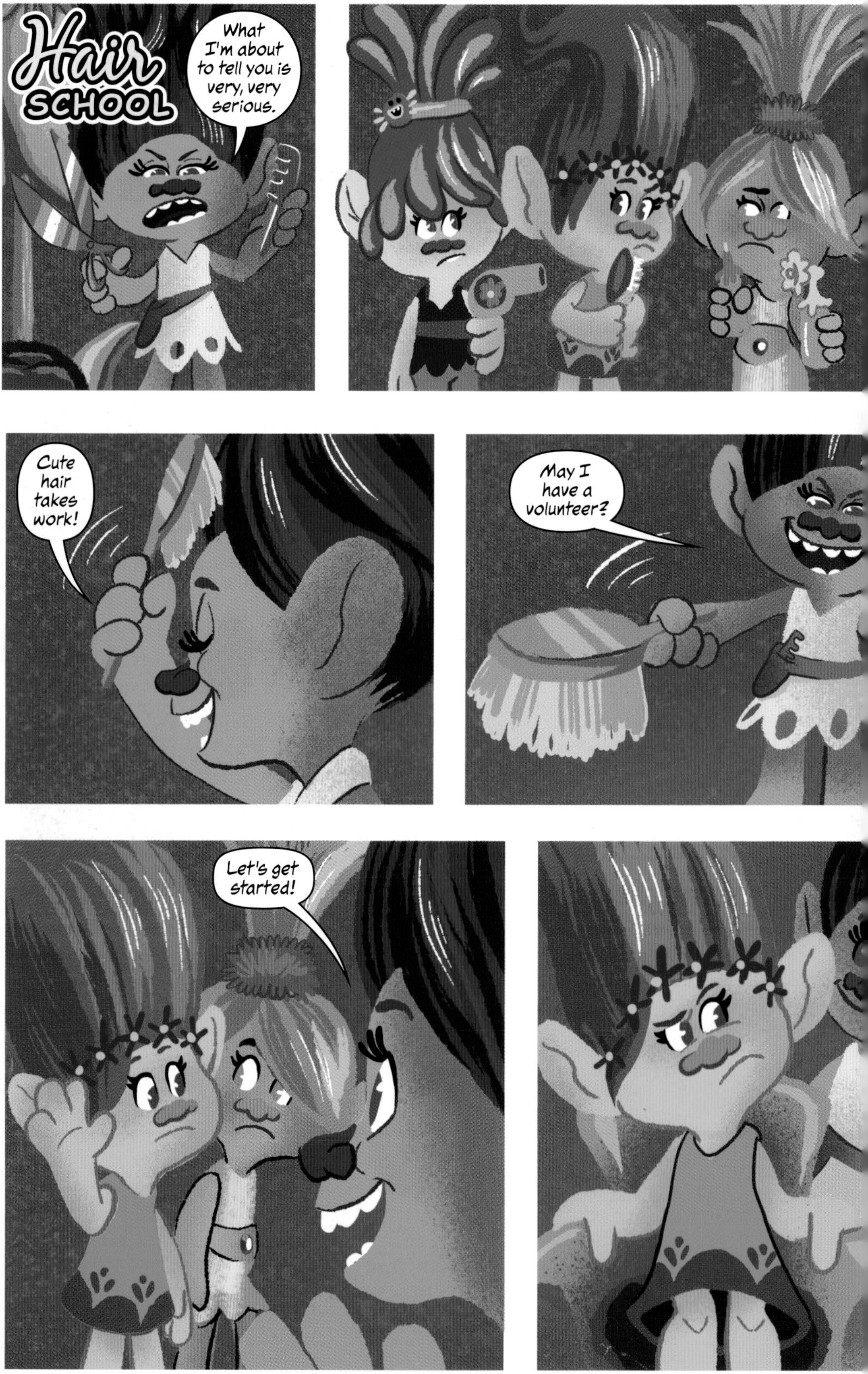
Hair School
What I'm about to tell you is very, very serious.
Cute hair takes work!
May I have a volunteer?
Let's get started!

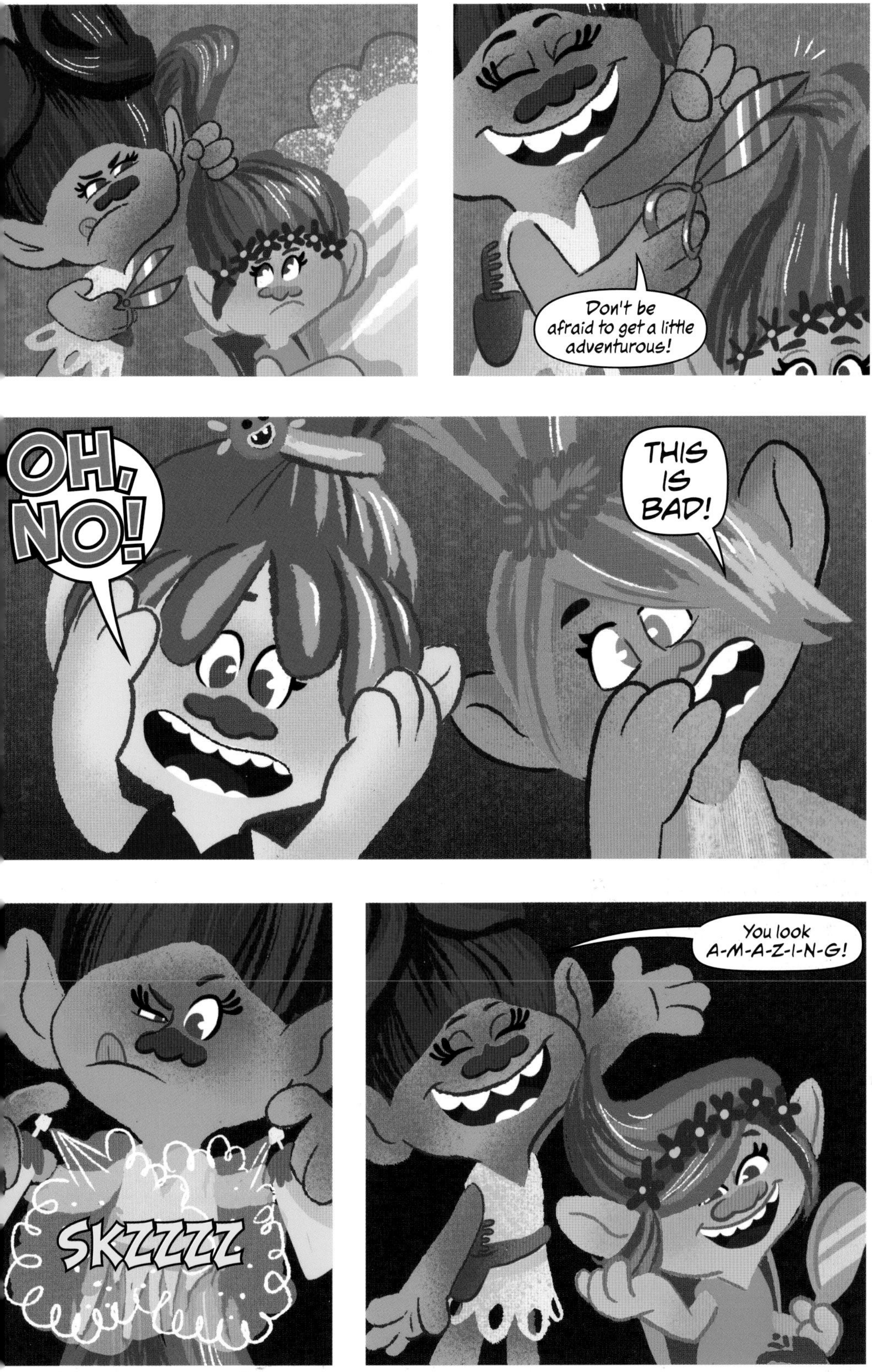
Don't be afraid to get a little adventurous!
OH, NO!
THIS IS BAD!
SKZZZZ
You look A-M-A-Z-I-N-G!

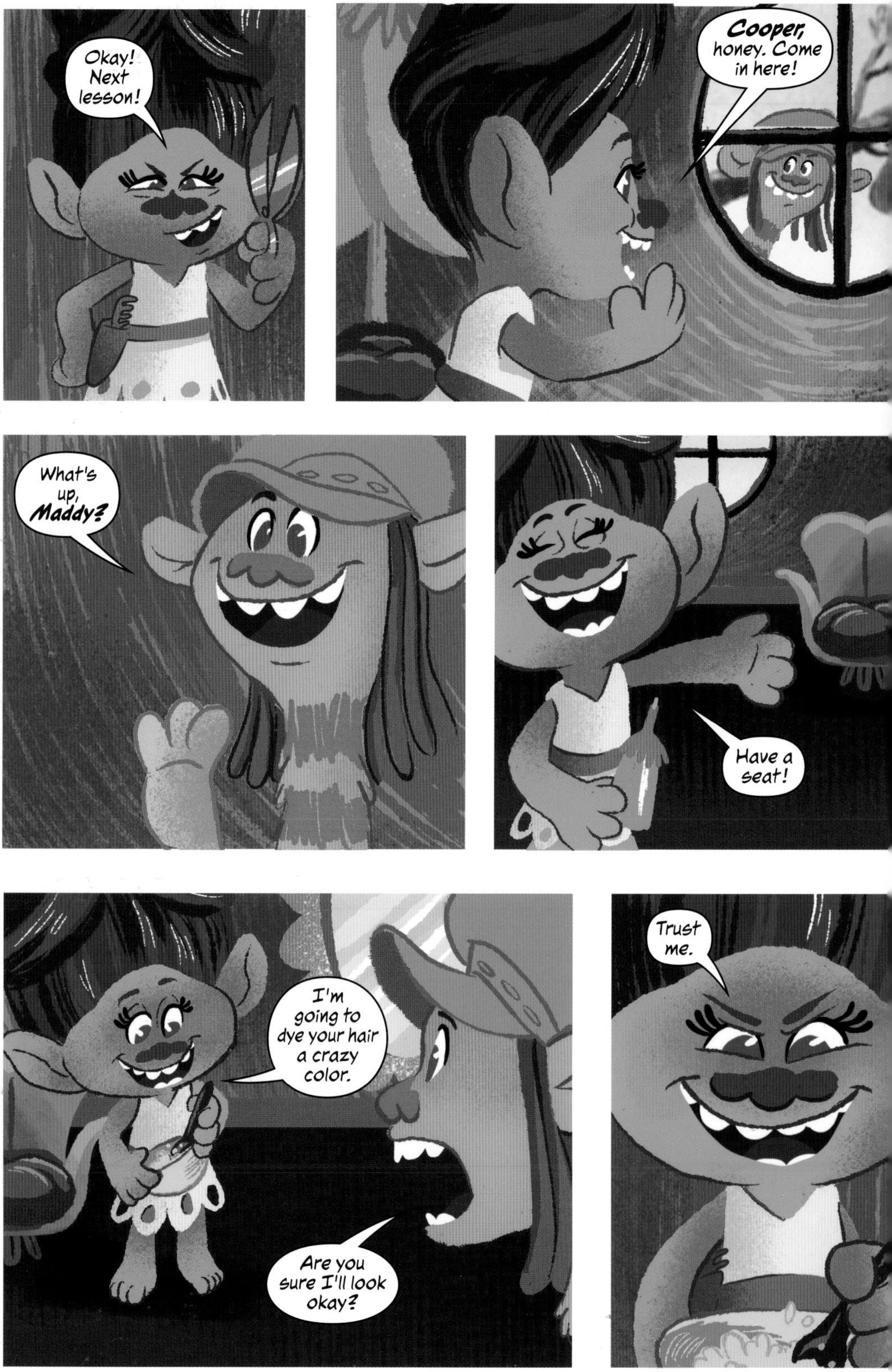
Okay! Next lesson!
Cooper, honey. Come in here!
What's up, Maddy?
Have a seat!
I'm going to dye your hair a crazy color.
Are you sure I'll look okay?
Trust me.

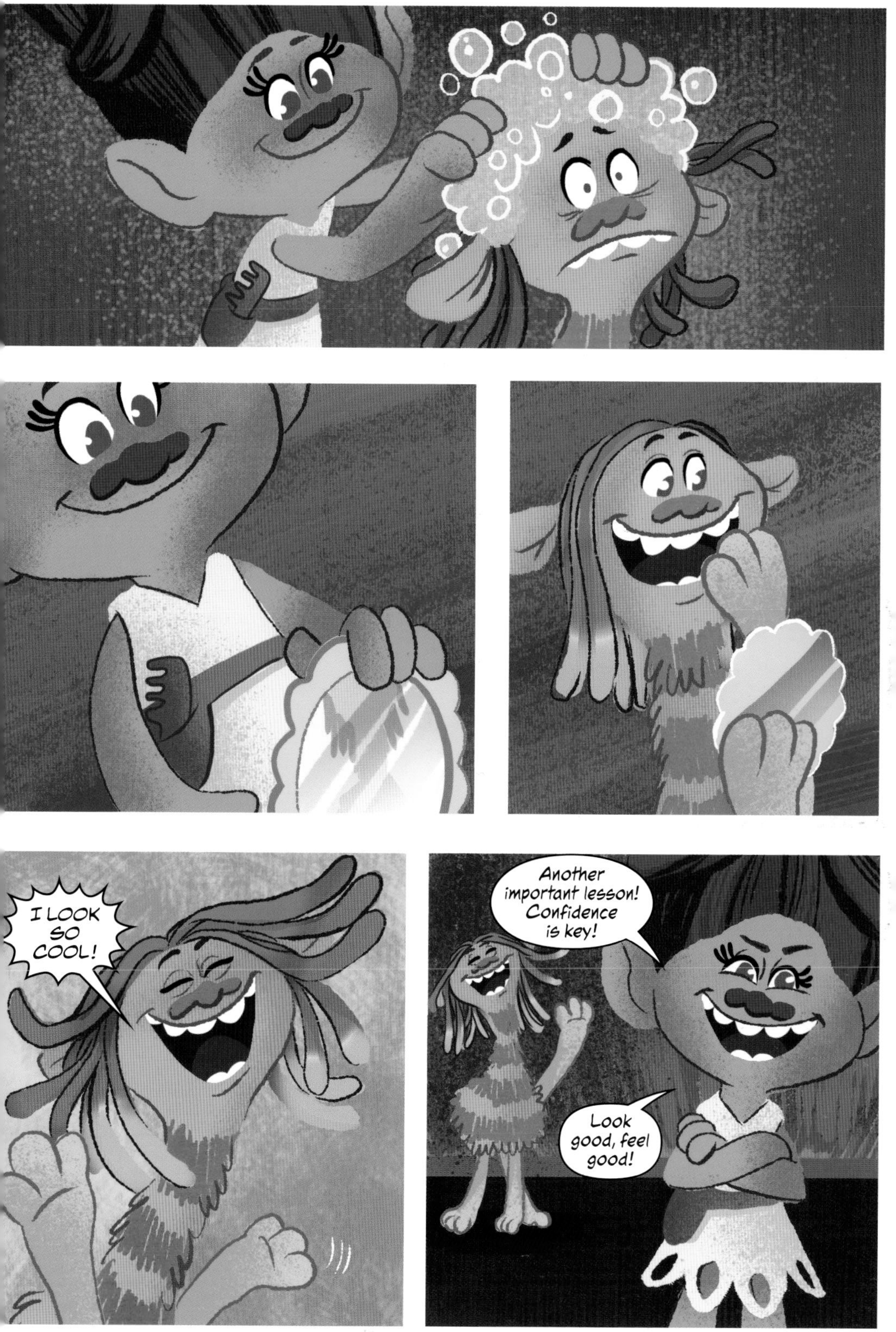
I LOOK SO COOL!
Another important lesson! Confidence is key!
Look good, feel good!

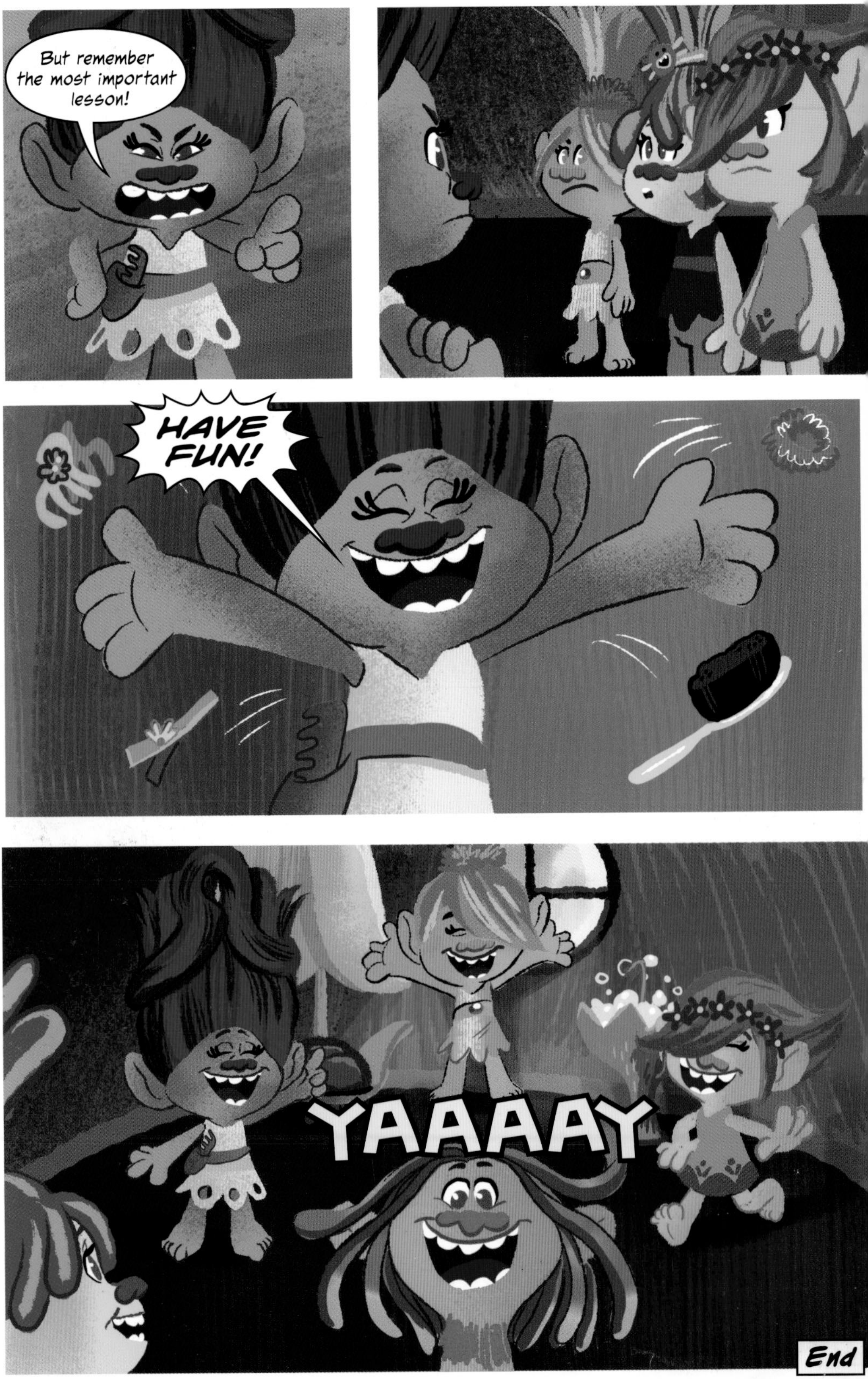
But remember the most important lesson!
HAVE FUN!
YAAAAY
End

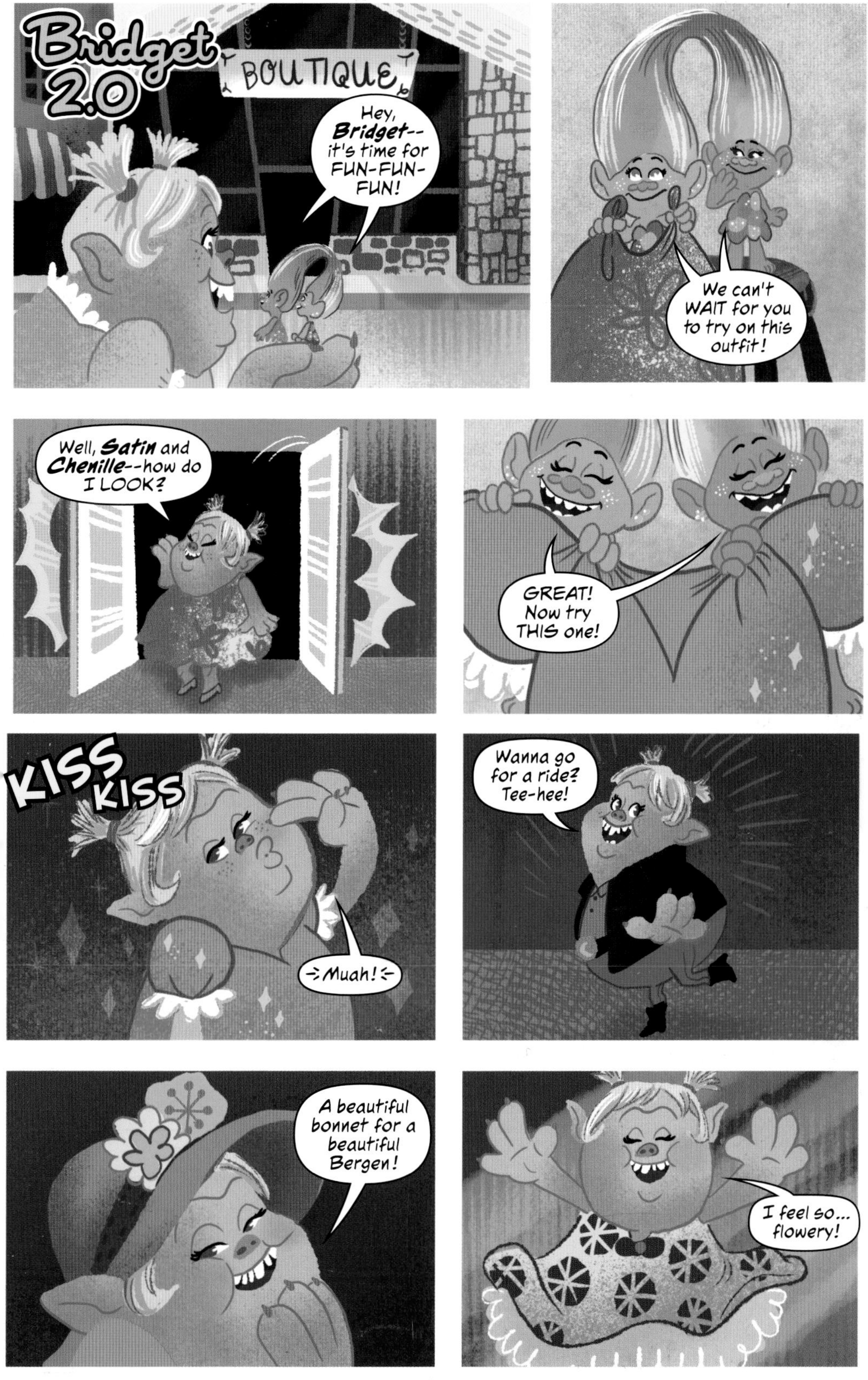
Bridget 2.0
BOUTIQUE
Hey, **Bridget**-- it's time for FUN-FUN-FUN!
We can't WAIT for you to try on this outfit!
Well, **Satin** and **Chenille**--how do I LOOK?
GREAT! Now try THIS one!
KISS KISS
Muah!
Wanna go for a ride? Tee-hee!
A beautiful bonnet for a beautiful Bergen!
I feel so... flowery!

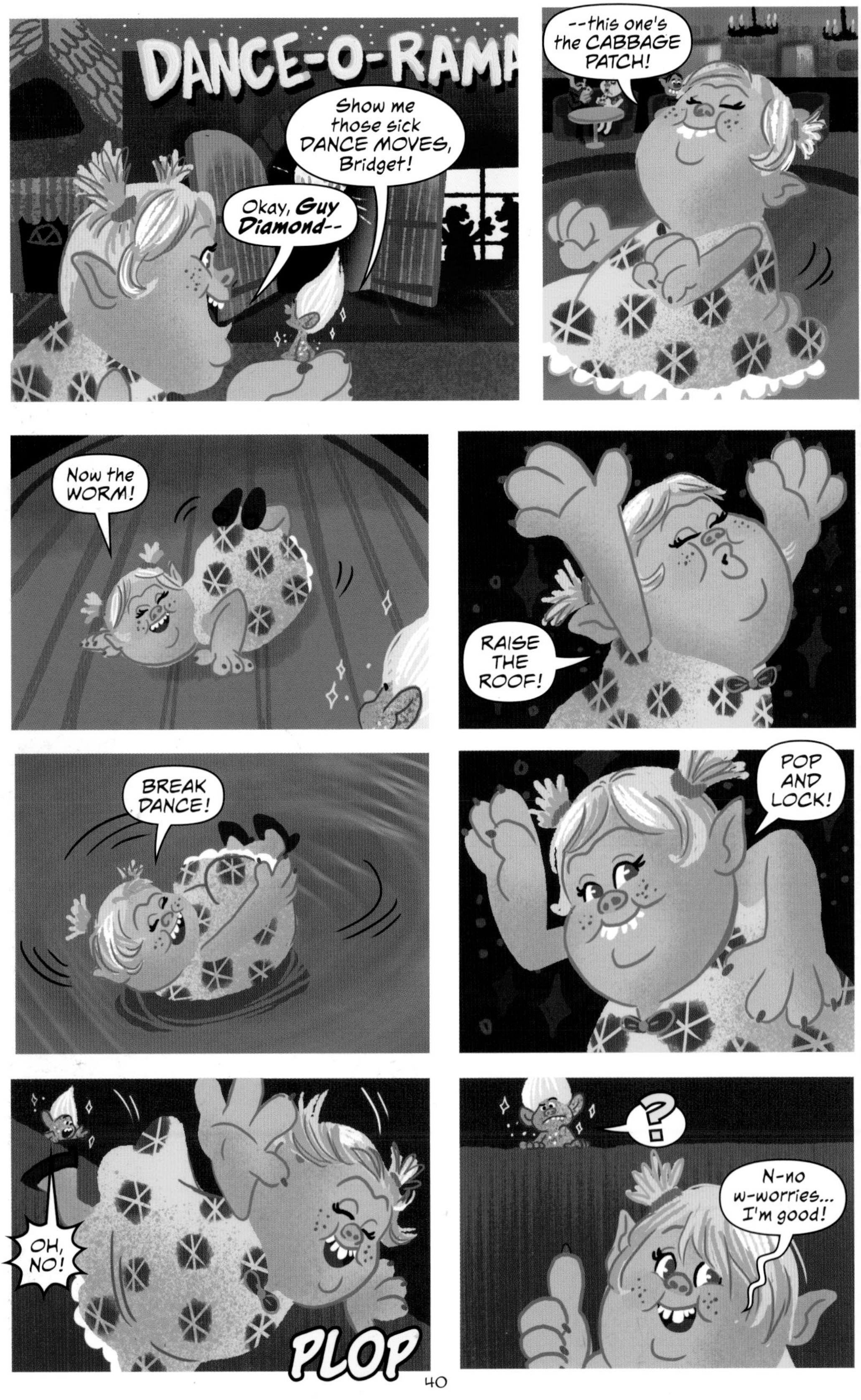
DANCE-O-RAMA
Show me those sick DANCE MOVES, Bridget!
Okay, Guy Diamond--
--this one's the CABBAGE PATCH!
Now the WORM!
RAISE THE ROOF!
BREAK DANCE!
POP AND LOCK!
OH, NO!
PLOP
?
N-no w-worries... I'm good!

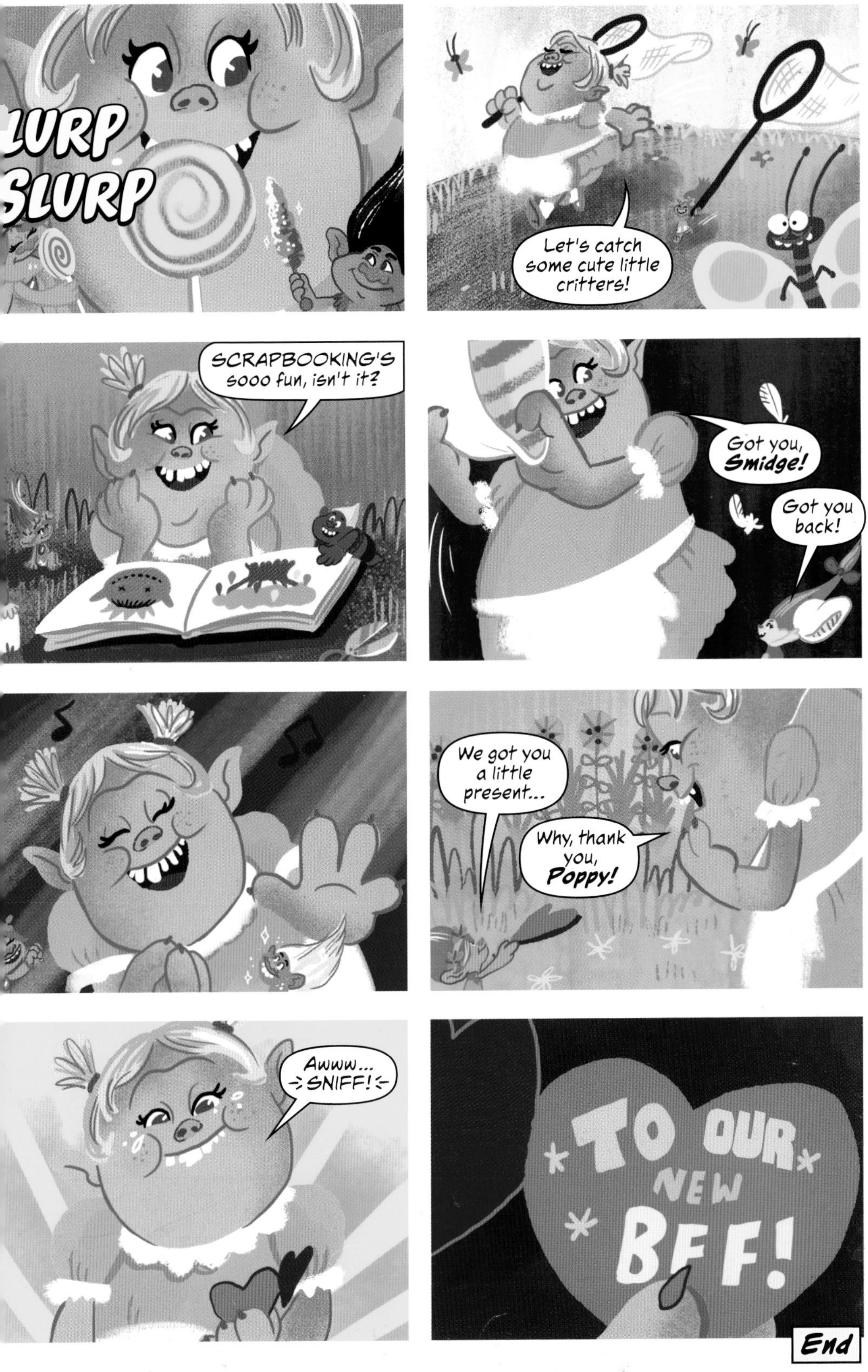
LURP
SLURP
Let's catch some cute little critters!
SCRAPBOOKING'S sooo fun, isn't it?
Got you, Smidge!
Got you back!
We got you a little present...
Why, thank you, Poppy!
Awww... SNIFF!
TO OUR NEW BFF!
End

SECRET MESSENGER

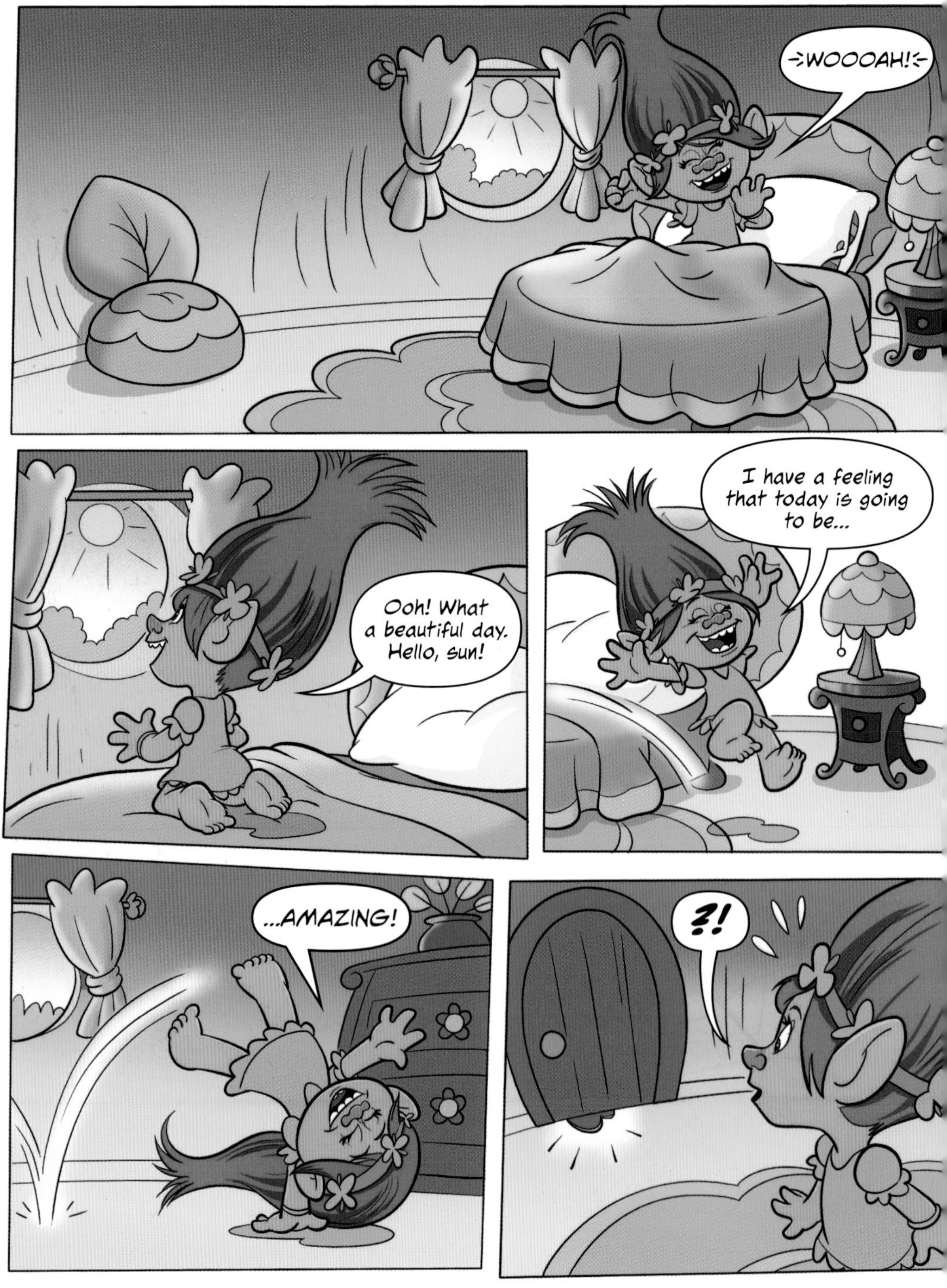
WOOOAH!
Ooh! What a beautiful day. Hello, sun!
I have a feeling that today is going to be...
...AMAZING!
?!

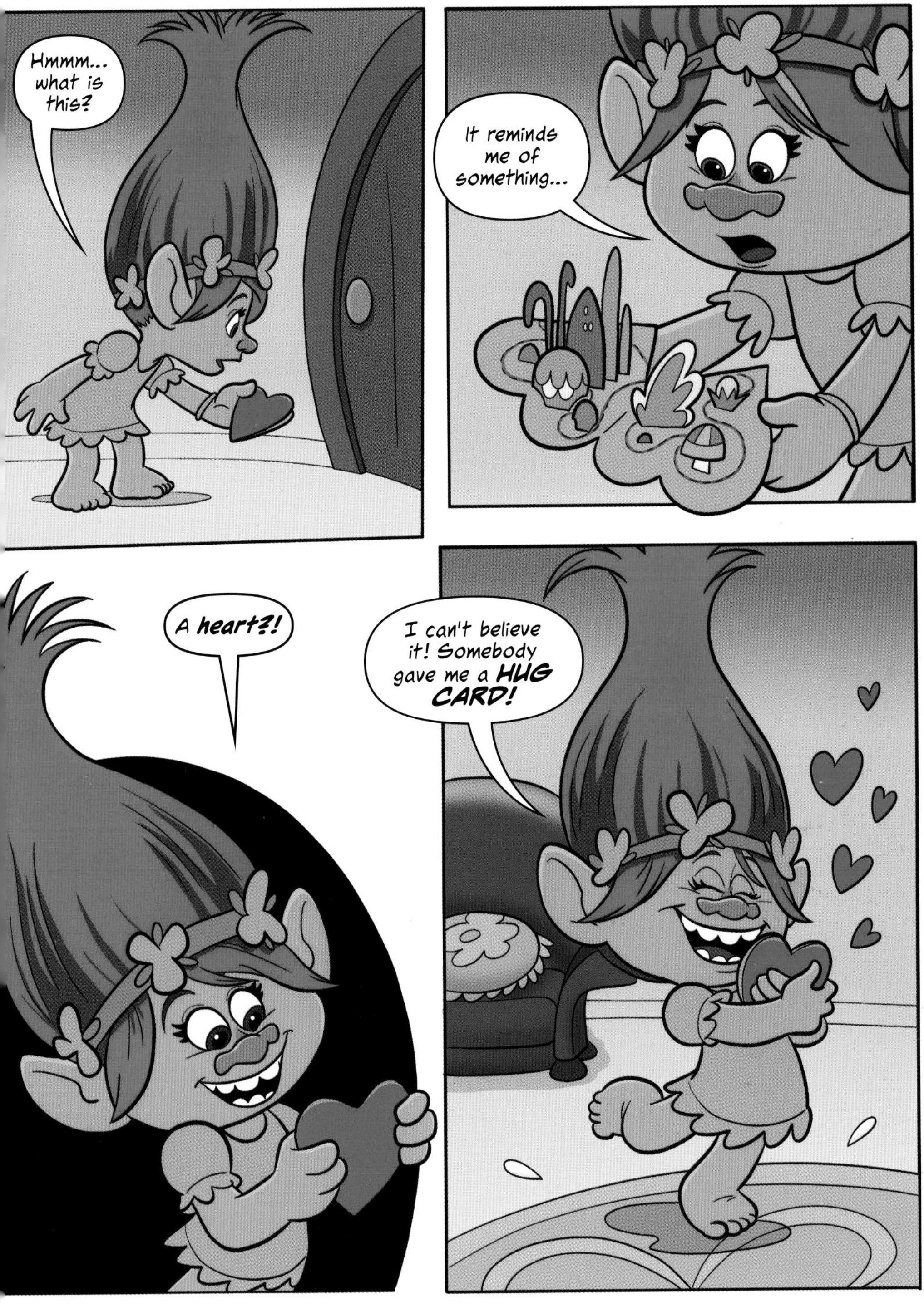
Hmmm... what is this?
It reminds me of something...
A heart?!
I can't believe it! Somebody gave me a HUG CARD!

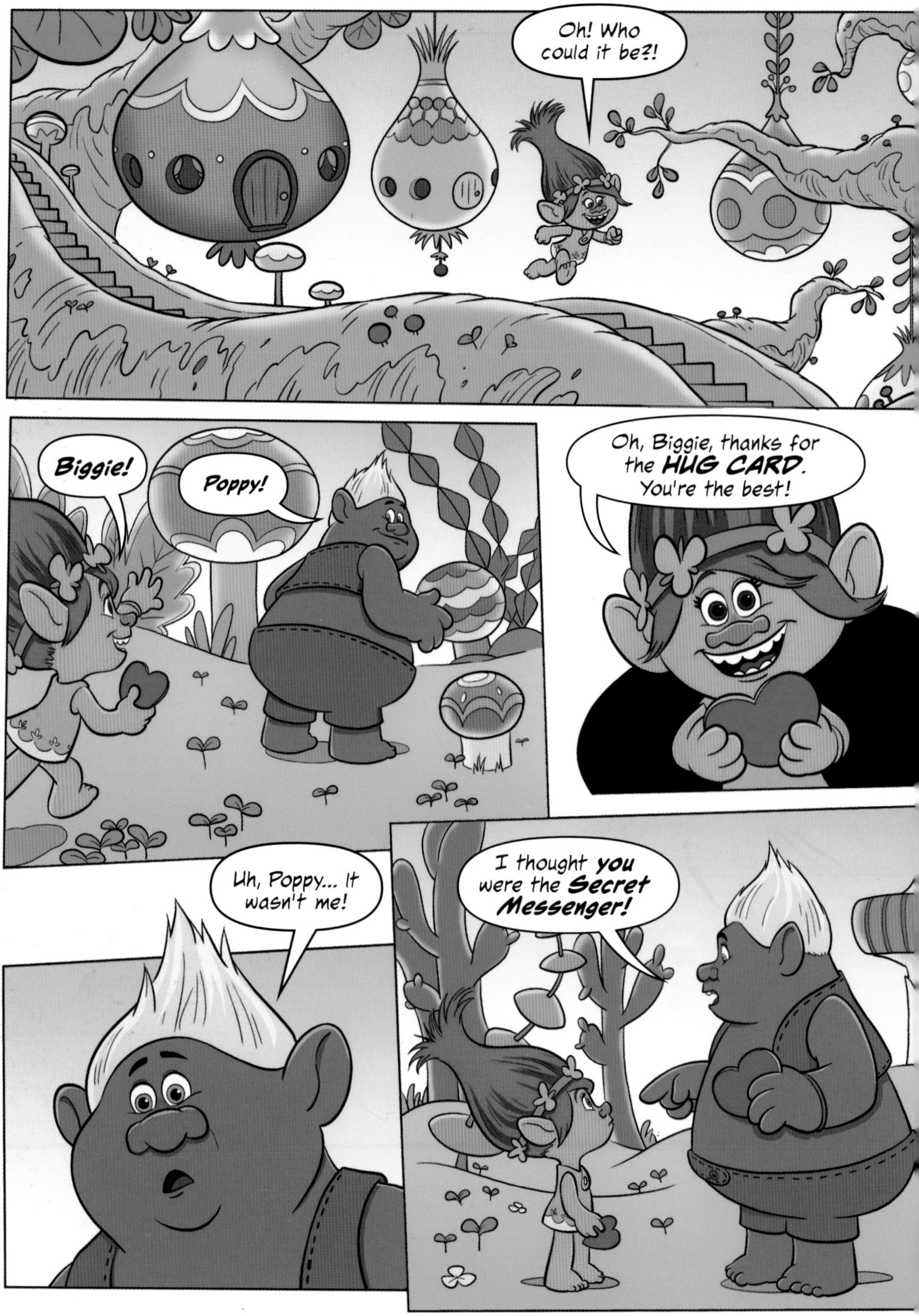
Oh! Who could it be?!
Biggie!
Poppy!
Oh, Biggie, thanks for the HUG CARD. You're the best!
Uh, Poppy... It wasn't me!
I thought you were the Secret Messenger!

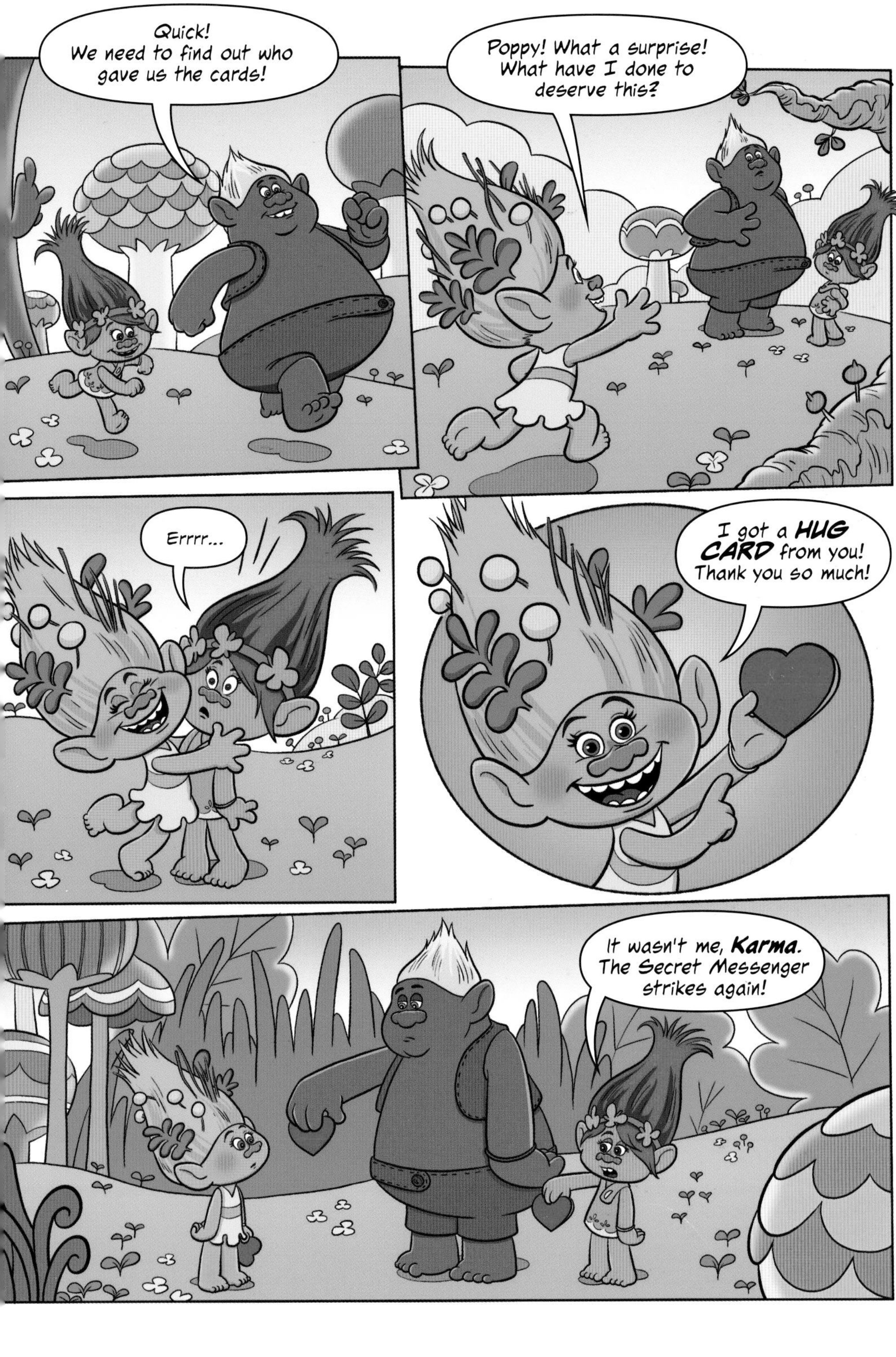
Quick! We need to find out who gave us the cards!
Poppy! What a surprise! What have I done to deserve this?
Errrr...
I got a **HUG CARD** from you! Thank you so much!
It wasn't me, **Karma**. The Secret Messenger strikes again!

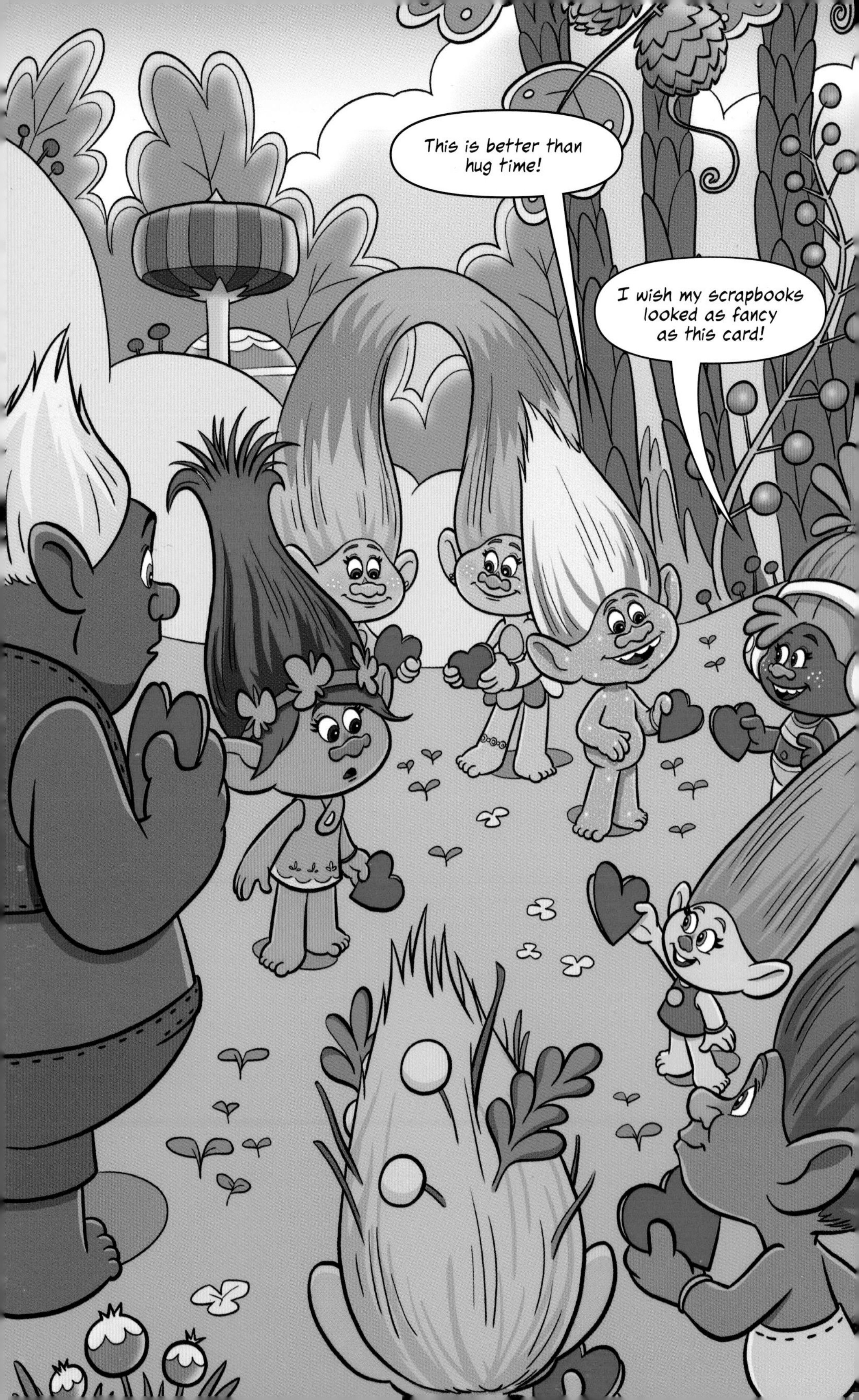
This is better than hug time!
I wish my scrapbooks looked as fancy as this card!

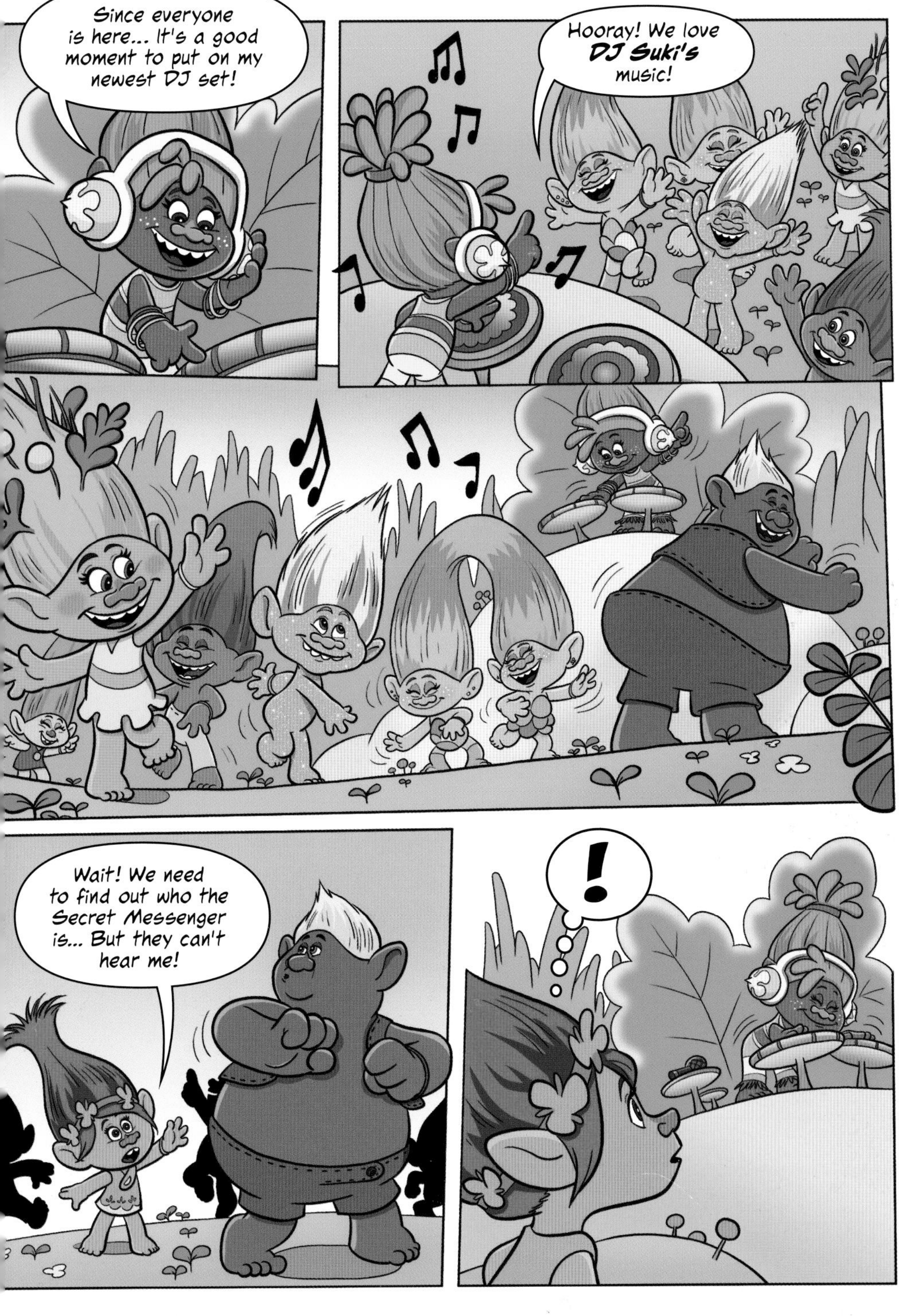
Since everyone is here... It's a good moment to put on my newest DJ set!
Hooray! We love DJ Suki's music!
Wait! We need to find out who the Secret Messenger is... But they can't hear me!
!

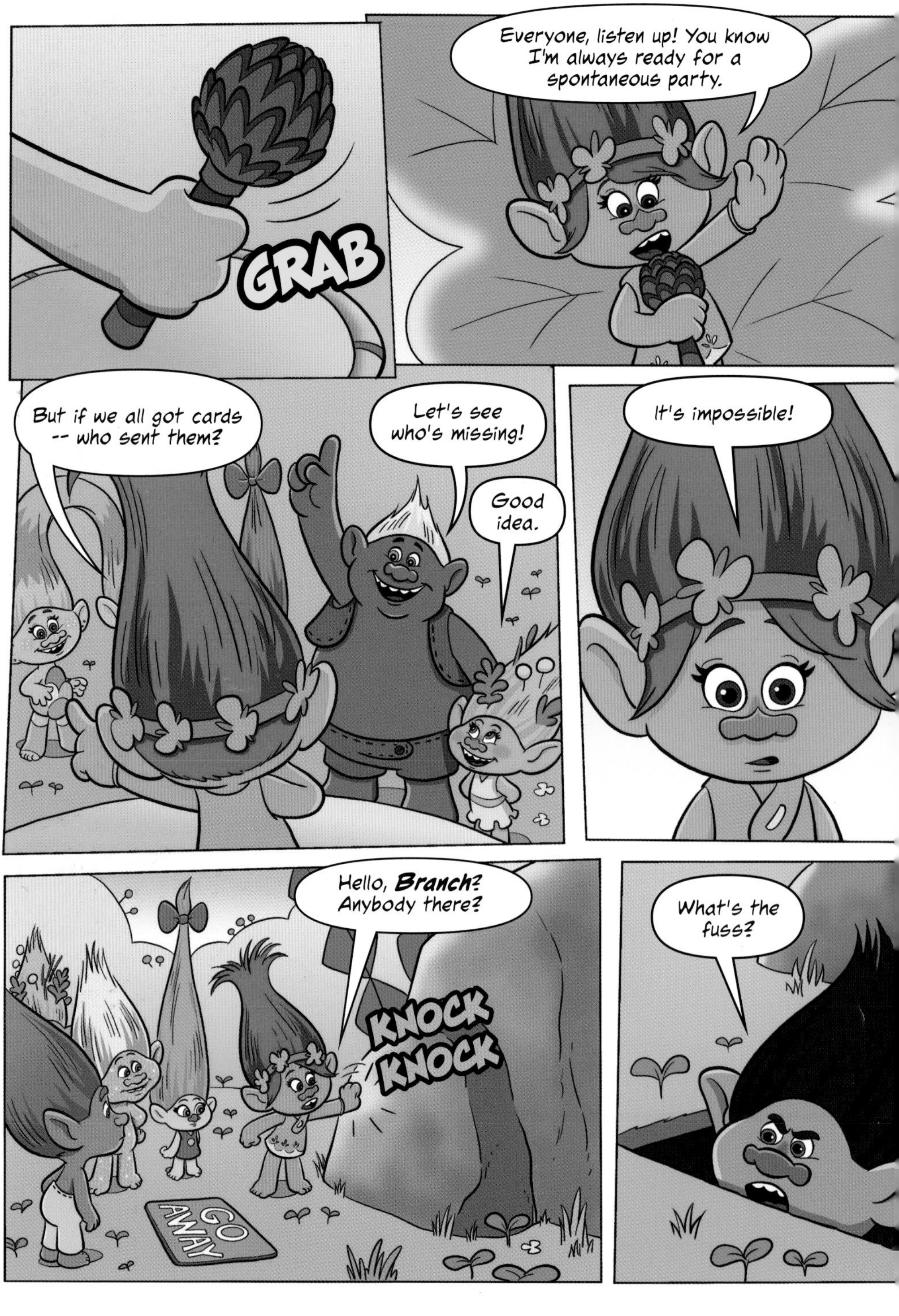
GRAB
Everyone, listen up! You know I'm always ready for a spontaneous party.
But if we all got cards -- who sent them?
Let's see who's missing!
Good idea.
It's impossible!
Hello, **Branch**? Anybody there?
KNOCK KNOCK
GO AWAY
What's the fuss?

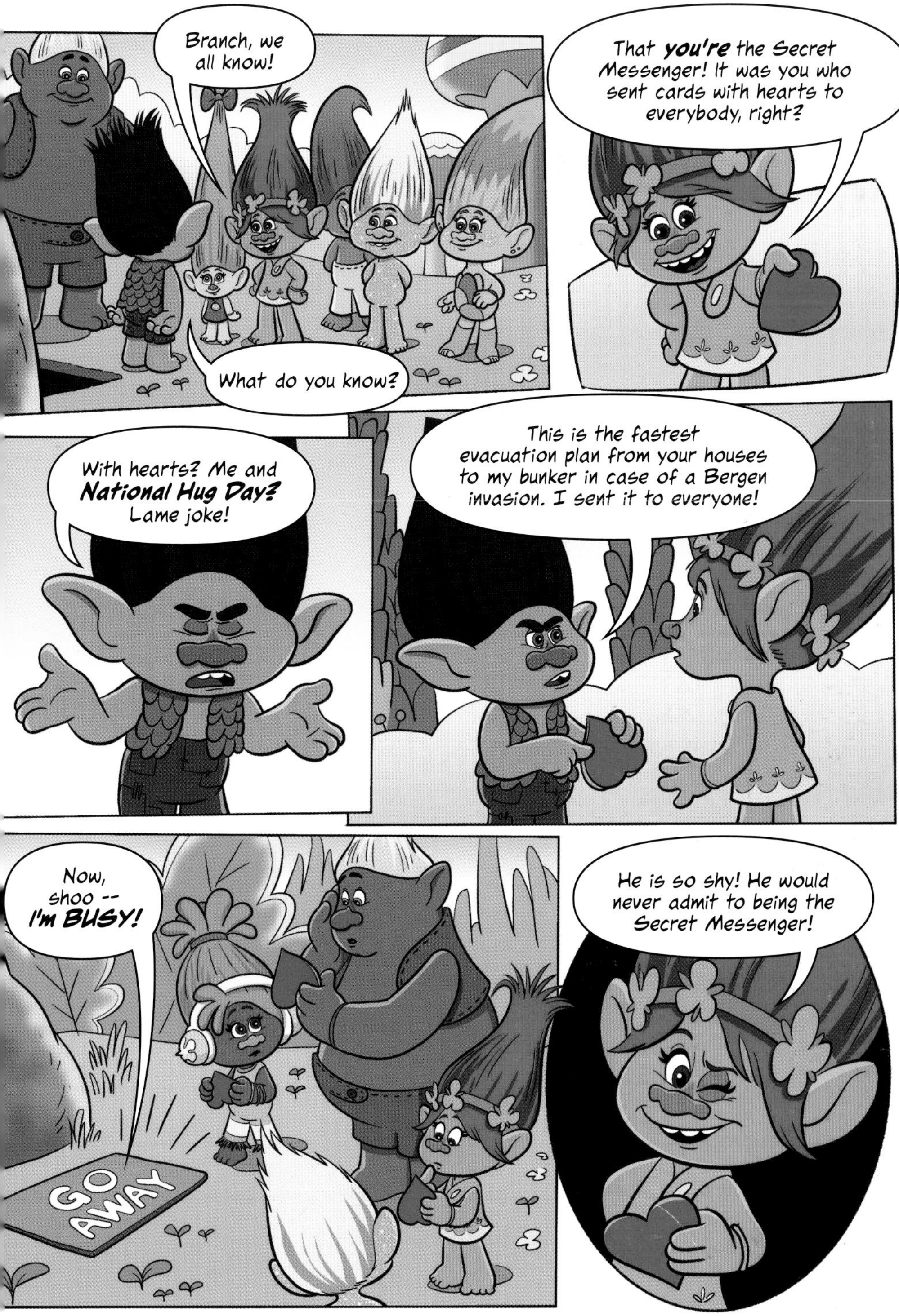
Branch, we all know!
What do you know?
That **you're** the Secret Messenger! It was you who sent cards with hearts to everybody, right?
With hearts? Me and **National Hug Day?** Lame joke!
This is the fastest evacuation plan from your houses to my bunker in case of a Bergen invasion. I sent it to everyone!
Now, shoo -- ***I'm BUSY!***
GO AWAY
He is so shy! He would never admit to being the Secret Messenger!

End

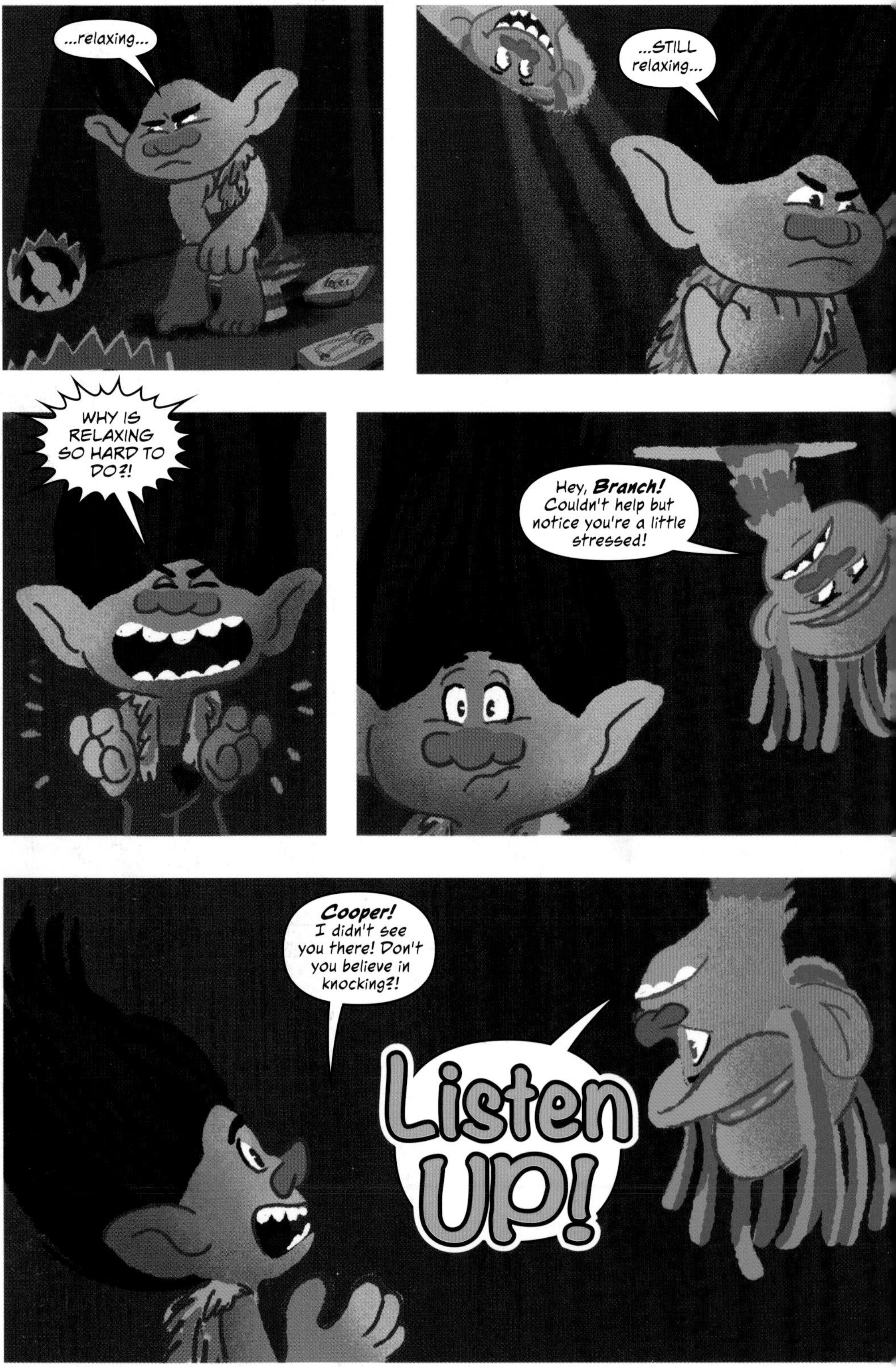
...relaxing...
...STILL relaxing...
WHY IS RELAXING SO HARD TO DO?!
Hey, **Branch!** Couldn't help but notice you're a little stressed!
Cooper! I didn't see you there! Don't you believe in knocking?!
Listen UP!

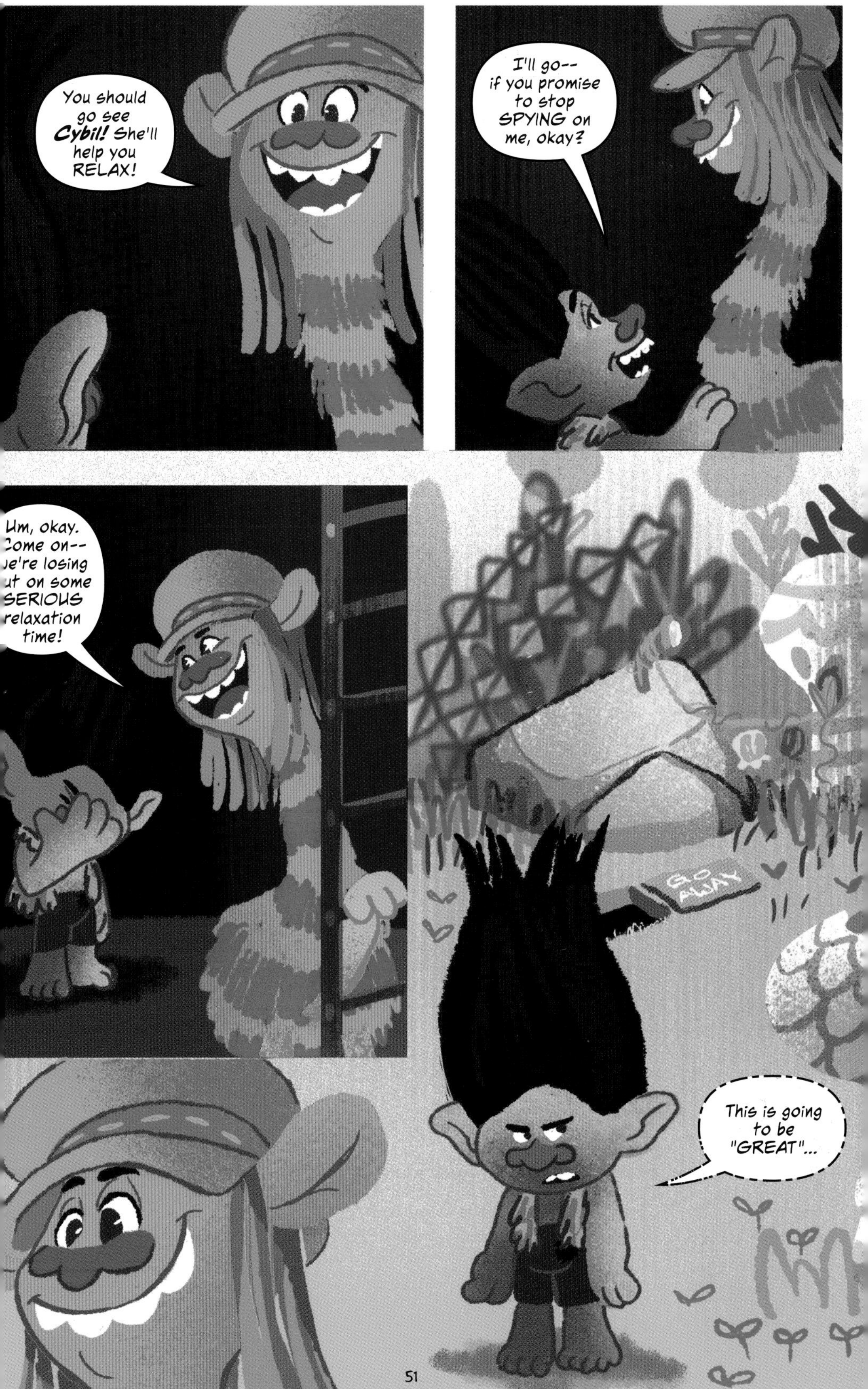
You should go see Cybil! She'll help you RELAX!
I'll go-- if you promise to stop SPYING on me, okay?
Um, okay. Come on-- we're losing out on some SERIOUS relaxation time!
GO AWAY
This is going to be "GREAT"...

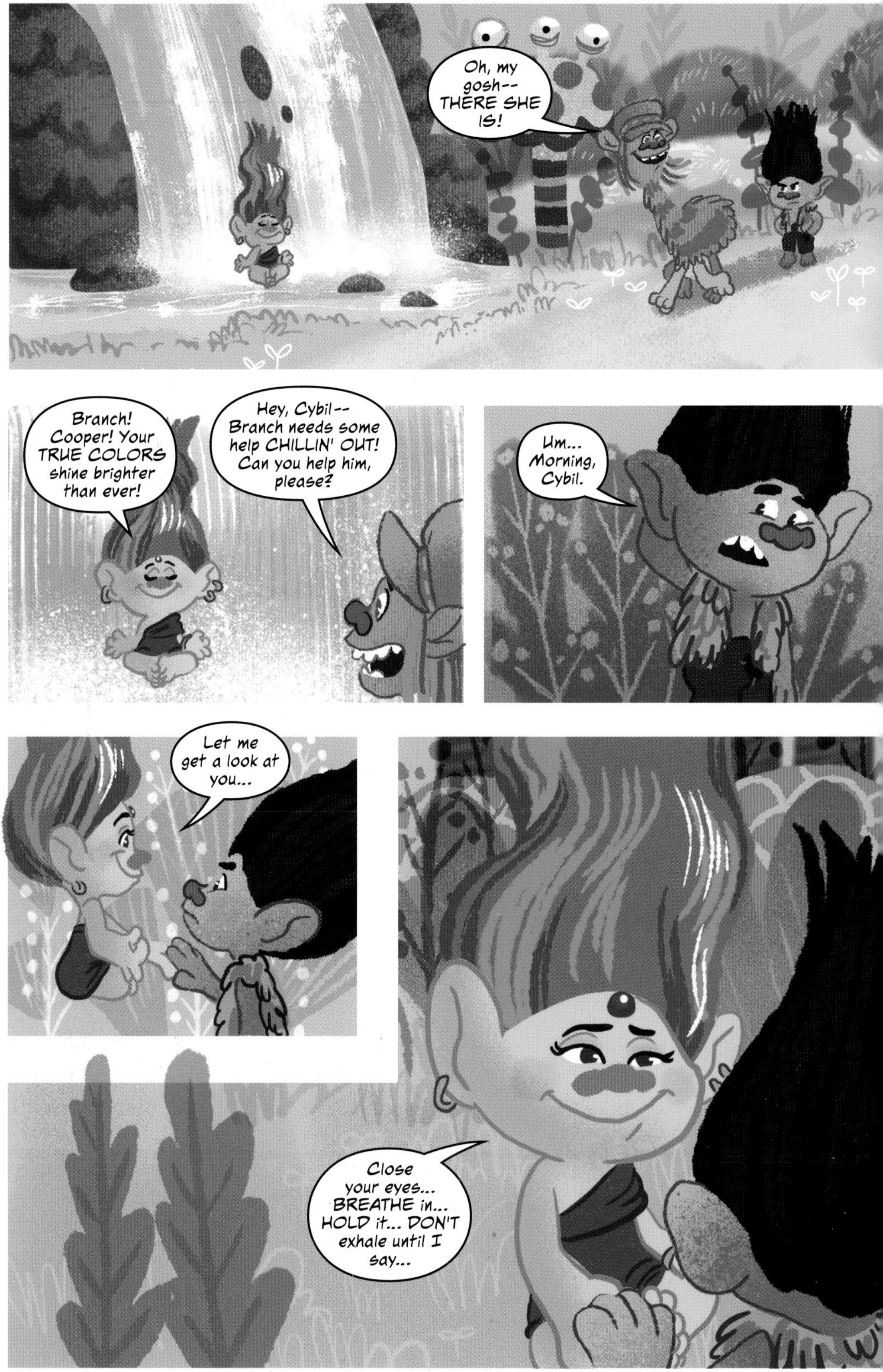

Oh, my gosh-- THERE SHE IS!
Branch! Cooper! Your TRUE COLORS shine brighter than ever!
Hey, Cybil-- Branch needs some help CHILLIN' OUT! Can you help him, please?
Um... Morning, Cybil.
Let me get a look at you...
Close your eyes... BREATHE in... HOLD it... DON'T exhale until I say...

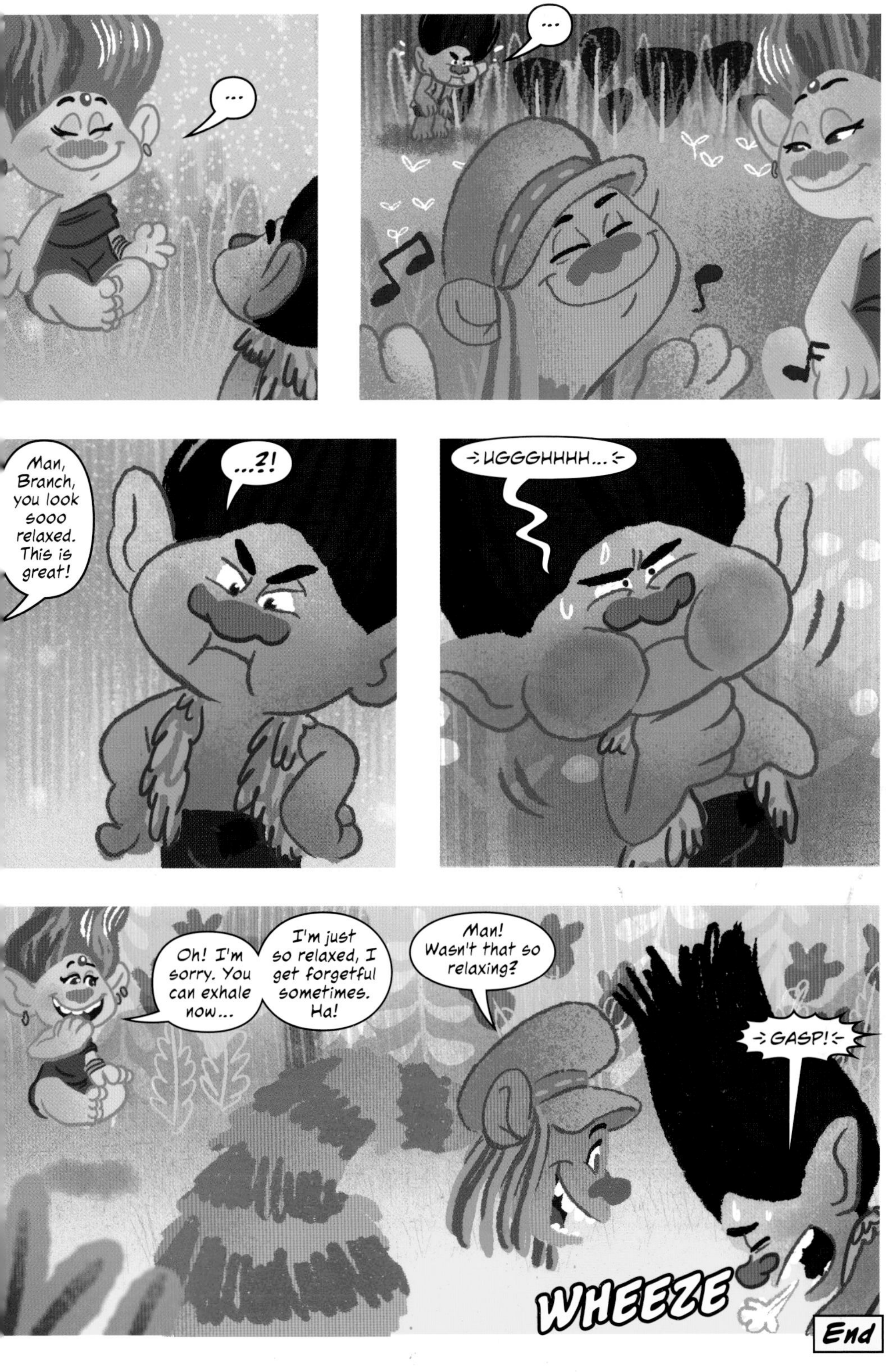
...
...
Man, Branch, you look sooo relaxed. This is great!
...?!
UGGGHHHH...
Oh! I'm sorry. You can exhale now...
I'm just so relaxed, I get forgetful sometimes. Ha!
Man! Wasn't that so relaxing?
GASP!
WHEEZE
End

MEET THE TROLLS

POPPY

Relentlessly upbeat, Poppy wields her positivity like a super-power! The heroic leader of the Trolls, Poppy always encourages her friends to believe that, with a song in your heart, you can do anything. Because when it comes to life, why say it when you can sing it?

FUN FACTS

Loves to sing
Eternally optimistic
Befriends all manner of little critters
Hugs her friends every hour, on the hour
Cherishes scrapbooking and crafting invitations
Knows everything sounds better with a cowbell
Brings everyone together, Troll or otherwise

MEET THE Trolls

SATIN & CHENILLE

Satin and Chenille are the most fashion-forward members of the Snack Pack, and their fashion knowledge is extensive, covering everything from haute couture runways to the latest street fashions. These twins are connected by a loop made of their brightly colored hair! Satin and Chenille are instrumental in putting together all of Poppy's various dresses and outfits.

FUN FACTS

Satin is the pink one; Chenille's the blue one
They're total BFFFs—Best Fashion Friends Forever
Four hands means quick costume changes during big
Troll Village events
These twins are all about independence;
They never ever wear the same outfit at the same time!

MEET THE Trolls

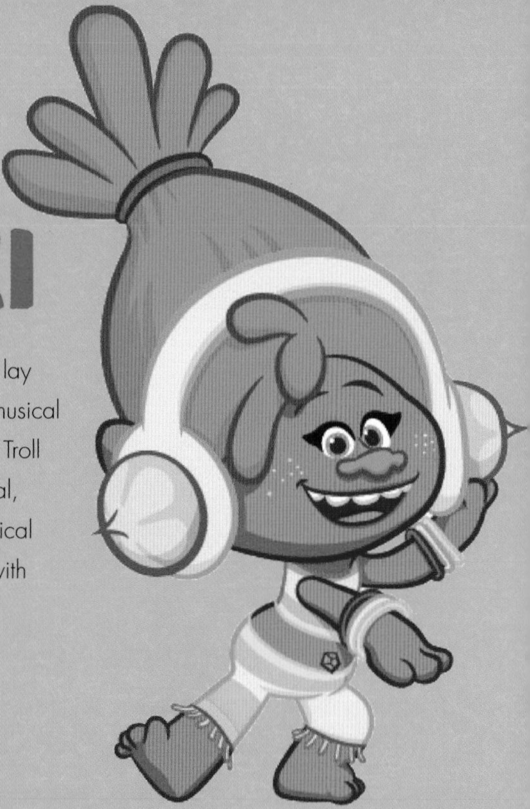

DJ SUKI

DJ Suki can always be counted on to lay down some beats for an impromptu musical moment—of which there are many in Troll Village. Her DJ equipment is all natural, consisting of various colorful and musical critters that she scratches and mixes with to create totally unique sounds.

FUN FACTS

- Troll Village's resident mash-up expert
- Wears headphones made of yarn
- Drops a needle-scratch noise during awkward moments
- Her playlist is always upbeat and up-tempo

MEET THE Trolls

HARPER

Harper believes that no canvas is too small when it comes to letting all her true colors shine! Her own hair is all Harper needs to express herself in every color imaginable. If a picture is worth a thousand words, then Harper can say…well, she can say a lot!

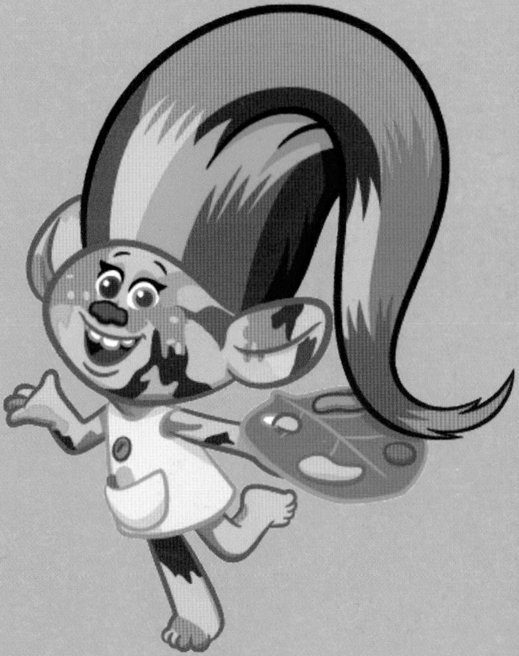

FUN FACTS

- Can speak, but would rather create than chat
- Uses her hair like a giant paintbrush
- Covered head-to-toe in paint…
- …except for her smock, which stays magically spotless

MEET THE Trolls

SMIDGE

Smidge is a teeny tiny Troll with a shockingly deep baritone voice. Her hobbies include: weightlifting, listening to Swedish heavy-metal music, and crocheting.

FUN FACTS

Incredibly disciplined when it comes to fitness and nutrition
Likes to fit in a quick workout during any dance number
Jumps rope and lifts dumbells with her own long hair

MEET THE BERGENS

KING GRISTLE

Following a very unhappy day in his childhood, King Gristle dedicated his rule to returning happiness to Bergen Town. Gristle is convinced that Trolls are the key to cheering up his people, and he may be right, but not in the way he expects!

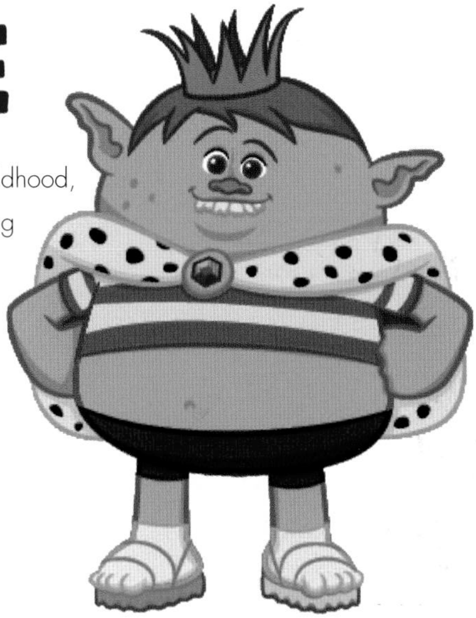

FUN FACTS

- Actually pretty good at busting rhymes
- Roller-skating is his secret talent
- His idea of a fancy date is going to Bergen Town's premier all-you-can-eat pizza buffet
- Will never sit down to a meal without a freshly pressed bib

MEET THE BERGENS

BRIDGET

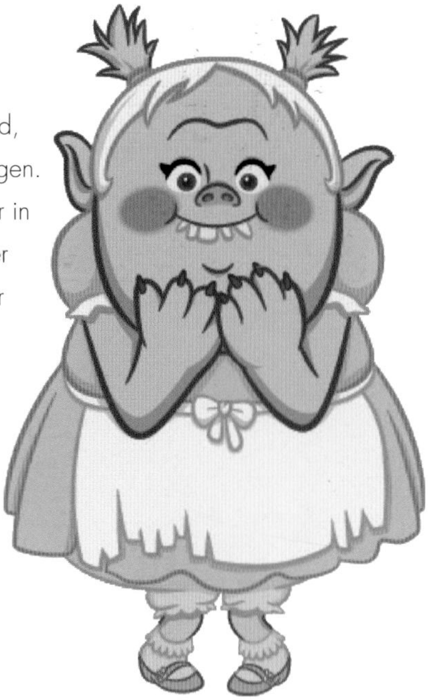

Sweet, sensitive, soft-spoken, and kind-hearted, Bridget is a world apart from every other Bergen. Stuck being the scullery maid and dishwasher in Bergen Town's Royal Kitchen, will Bridget ever find someone to love her inner self and let her true colors shine?

FUN FACTS

- Believes in herself, but unsure how to communicate that to others
- Treats everyone with respect, even if she doesn't get any
- Secretly romantic
- Wants to find happiness in a way that's different from other Bergens